THE UNFORESEEN
SHORT STORIES

VANDANA
SRIVASTAVA

INDIA • SINGAPORE • MALAYSIA

ISBN 979-8-88935-994-4

For Tanay, Tarush & Pragya

*Take a walk with a turtle and
behold the world in pause!*

Bruce Feiler

CONTENTS

Innocence

It was an exceptionally bright afternoon, the sun was scorching. Golden flames leapt out from the hot core, like fire from a dragon's mouth. At least that's how it looked to the little boy standing in the middle of the pavement, hands on hips, neck turned up to the sky.

He looked right at the sun, or rather, he tried. His eyes squinted, they played games with him. They tried to run away from his head, they almost screamed at him. "Look away, it hurts!" But the boy was curious. He wanted to capture the brilliant intensity of the ball of fire with his reluctant eyes.

After a few seconds, he relented and glanced around him. The old man sauntering alongside had his gaze firmly on the footpath ahead. The lady across the road with a large bag on her shoulder was busy looking for something important inside it. And the young man rushing to his car put on his sunglasses with one hand as he fumbled for his keys with the other, blocking the sun right out.

The little boy then decided that maybe the sun being so bright was not such a big deal after all. Nobody else seemed to be working as hard as him to look at it. And anyway, it hurt. So he blinked his eyes a couple of times and walked on home. His smart blue shorts smelled nice. His cream cotton shirt perfectly ironed. White socks and shiny black shoes. His bag slung casually over one shoulder.

An angel, no less!

***

She looked at her screen saver, her eyes hurt and her head was in a mood swing of its own. Late nights and successive early mornings can have that impact on the senses. Deadlines were such bummers, as were school runs.

But the image of her eight year old made her smile. He was flashing his fake cheeky grin, balancing at least ten books of all sizes on his head while trying to kick a football in the air, a mixed bundle of joy and exhaustion.

Propped up snugly with at least five cushions on the sofa and her legs stretched out on a chair, she dreaded the thought of having to get up and clean the room. But it was a huge mess and it had to be done. Clothes, stationary, leftovers from breakfast, it looked like a tornado had made a surprise visit to the living room. She could even smell herself now and a shower was extremely inviting but the effort to get up was equally overwhelming. The yin yang of life.

Putting the laptop aside she wished for a magic wand that could make the clutter vanish with a sweep of her hand. Before she got lost in what else her imaginary wand could do, she blinked her eyes a couple of times, swept her curly, black hair up in a bun, took a deep breath, and got on with it. Better to finish up before the little monster came home and made it impossible to do anything other than chase after him.

The devil, no less!

***

As he prepared to leap across the huge puddle on the path, he saw his reflection. His slickly combed hair reminded him of Mom. She made sure they stayed in place by patting his head umpteen times accompanied by the insistent reminder. 'Keep them that way!'.

But his focus went back to the more important things in life. To see if he could jump that far and clear the puddle in one leap. As he landed, almost, right across the puddle, the reminder was a distant memory. And as his shoes splashed in the mucky brown water, he couldn't be bothered to notice that they had turned a shade of brown as well. All he cared to see was if he had cleared the puddle.

Not satisfied with his performance, he walked right back and jumped again. This time even his socks turned brown. Not one to give up, he attempted it yet again. And this time, voila, his feet hit solid ground.

He looked around with a smile on his face but there was no one applauding him. Yet the little boy was keen to share his triumph. He spotted a mangy dog near the sidewall who seemed to be wagging his tail in appreciation at him. So he did a quick bow to the lone audience. For a moment he was tempted to discuss his achievement with Mangy but then remembered that he had to reach home on time. Although the why eluded him. But Mangy looked at him beseechingly. As if he too had tried so many times to jump across that puddle and never succeeded.

How could the boy not share his secret skills with the poor dog and deprive him of such pleasures in life. So he squatted on the pavement next to Mangy and had the most serious conversation of his life. He was imparting valuable knowledge. And Mangy was a great student, he sat there with his tongue hanging out, tail flat on the floor, listening attentively, pawing him gently once in a while. The boy made sure he told him everything properly and precisely.

Mangy gave a meek yelp at the end of the lecture, which the boy took as a note of thanks. And off he ran, not noticing how crumpled his shorts and shirt had become after all that jumping, crouching, and squatting. And not to mention, the dog hair and saliva that Mangy had so benevolently bestowed upon him.

***

She sat on the floor reading the letter for the second time. She had spotted it amongst his numerous indecipherable sketches that lay all over the floor. He loved to draw even if it took ages to figure out what was staring back at you from the papers. As she scrutinised one that was possibly meant to be a horse but looked more like a cross between a cow and a dog, she spotted the letter popping out from behind it. The gloomy words leapt out in contrast to the cheerful hybrid.

She wondered how he had forgotten to give it to her as she read it for the third time. Not that it was anything new. He hardly remembered anything to do with school unless asked. But this was unacceptable. The letter from the Principal talked about all kinds of things. She desperately searched for some words that may have been a saving grace, something positive. But nothing in the letter went in that much desired direction.

His performance, his behaviour, his attitude, the list was endless. All his shortcomings in such detail. He seemed to be causing trouble in every possible way. They had written that they could not accept such underperforming and unfocused children in their school and a decision had to be taken.

She had let him off the hook often enough. She regretted having been so lenient with him. She glanced back at her screensaver and quickly looked away. It was time to get serious and make some changes. It was time to make him grow up.

Determinedly, she started gathering the papers off the floor. The hybrid cow-dog was on top of the stack and it didn't look at her approvingly. She slammed the damning letter right on top of it, unable to meet its eyes.

***

He liked looking at the mango tree he crossed daily on his way home. Unlike the grown-ups, it wasn't the mangoes that held his gaze. It was the twisted mangle of branches that caught his attention. His legs itched to swing from the ones high above. But he was scared of heights, a fact he admitted only to his pillow at night.

He watched as a large brown cat sauntered past him and jumped up on the first branch with grace and ease. It was the lowest one and she settled on it looking at him with challenging eyes. Or maybe it was an invitation to follow her he thought when she let out a soft meow. Flinging his bag on the ground, the little boy decided this was the day.

Placing his hands carefully at the right spots and taking a firm grip, he made it to the first branch and settled right next to Meow. Having had her fill of relaxing at this lower level of achievement, she decided to move higher in life. After imparting a few instructional purrs to him, she jumped on to the next branch. Although it was not too high up, the boy looked down in fear.

Meow kept standing on the branch above looking at him, she might have extended her paw to help if he had asked but he wanted to do this on his own. In a moment of quick decision, he scrambled on his feet and throwing his arms out, flung himself onto the next branch. Having conquered his fear, his joy knew no bounds. As he pumped his fists in celebration he lost hold and fell straight down to the grass below.

Meow jumped effortlessly on her four feet next to him while he lay sprawled on his back, a big smile on his face. He had observed her intently from his flat position and he knew how to do it better the next time, even the fall.

Grabbing a mango that had accompanied him on the way down, he rubbed the dirt off with his sleeve and stuffed it in his bag. He gave a knowing wink to Meow as he rushed home to give his Mom her favourite fruit.

****

Chocolate chip cookies were his favourite. She was planning a cookie theme for his upcoming birthday. Her mind went back to when he was younger and had climbed on the table to grab a cookie. His pudgy hands couldn't handle the plate and losing his balance, he fell right off the table and hurt his head. She had freaked out, worried, and fussed over him. She had even scolded him unreasonably in her paranoid state.

She often wondered if the trigger to his fear of heights had been the fall or her paranoia. But that's what parents needed to do. Save their children even if it meant scaring them. And he needed it right now, saving. Her approach was justified. Even if there was a fine line between scaring and scarring.

And now she would have to cancel the whole birthday plan. This wasn't the time to indulge him. Even if the cookies were made of broccoli, he didn't deserve them let alone chocolate chip ones.

****

Nearing his house, the little boy's eyes fell on a blossom of flowers. This time the eyes were happy and they did not want to run away. In fact, in addition to the bright red flowers, they also spotted a strange green creature and that made them want to stay even more. The boy wasn't sure what it was, a grasshopper, a praying mantis, or a creature from Mars! But he didn't think about that for too long. All he wanted to do was to catch it.

As his hands flashed out to grab it, the green thing hopped onto the next bush. The boy gathered all his patience and stood still to let Green Thing relax. And then he went for it again, with all his might and speed. He went right through the bushes and came out the other side. His fist curled around Green Thing. Success, yet again!

The twigs, branches, and thorns from the bush made cuts and bruises on his limbs but all he could think of was that he had to be gentle with the bug. So he relaxed his grip and let Green Thing loosen up a bit. He observed it for a while. He was almost tempted to give it a lecture on jumping too but decided this was expecting too much. Mangy was definitely much smarter than Green Thing. This guy would never get it, his brain was too small.

So he focused on analysing the creature and memorising everything about it. Long legs like his

Dad, the green colour as of his favourite blanket, and big black eyes like his Mom. It was oddly still and made no attempts to jump anymore, it probably understood that it was part of a ground-breaking experiment and decided to cooperate in the hope of achieving fame and fortune in return.

After putting in all the detailed features into his memory and deciding to 'Google up' on the bug, the little boy placed him back gently on a big shiny leaf and waved goodbye.

***

Her fingers drummed at the table, completely out of rhythm. She kept staring at the papers on it. She would wait right at the door for him, ready to pounce. If she didn't do it now he would surely sneak away, as would her steely resolve. She started pacing right in front of the door. She had to catch him as he entered.

Her phone rang endlessly, the peppy ring tone matching her strides back n forth, but surely not in sync with her mood. The notes met her ears and shattered into small pieces and then vanished into the air like puffs of smoke. Her thoughts were only for her son and him alone.

She couldn't afford to be gentle with him. He needed to understand, his wild ways needed to be curbed. And it wouldn't work with a soft hand.

She made a list in her head, of things he wouldn't be allowed to do. Of restrictions and bans and limits. Her steps hastened as she furiously dwelt on the rules that had to be laid down for him.

Her bun unravelled at the same pace as her thoughts. Her hair, along with many other things, was a mess by the time the doorbell rang.

****

The boy rang the doorbell as he thought of his adventures on the way home. Quite a fruitful day it had been. He had looked straight at the sun, managed to jump over a huge puddle, given Mangy a lecture, overcome his fear of heights, and then he had caught that mysterious bug, whose name he would find out soon. The size of the satisfied grin on his face would have put the Cheshire Cat to shame.

Curiosity, persistence, alertness, sensitivity, hard work...you name it...he had it!

His Mom opened the door. She looked at him. She saw his messed up hair, his crumpled clothes, his dirty shoes and socks. The many cuts and bruises all over his arms and legs looked almost like a pattern on his skin. Somehow she missed the huge and obvious grin.

He waited patiently. He wanted her to ask questions, he wanted to share his experiences with her. And the mango, he felt like he had some treasure hidden in his bag, that he couldn't wait to hand over to his Mom and see her smile.

She had questions for him, so many, about his marks, his teachers, his behaviour in class, and more. And when she saw the state he was in, the dirt and the mess, it infuriated her even more. The words from the letter floated in front of her eyes and deepened her frown.

Careless, inattentive, lazy, hyperactive, troublemaker...you name it....it was on the list!

But he was adamant. He did not let the grin go and looked straight into her eyes. He knew she would notice, she would ask. He knew she wanted to know. The success of his achievements depended on her stamp of approval.

And magic happened. Her eyes played games too. They suddenly refused to look at the clothes, the hair, the shoes. They darted right onto that beautiful happy grin. The slightly chipped tooth made it look even cuter. And the only question that came to her mind was, "What have you been up to my baby?" And as she asked, she ruffled his hair, messing it up even further, and matched his grin, ear to ear.

He threw his bruised and battered arms around her neck and started telling his stories. She hugged him tight listening with rapt attention. The door slammed shut behind them as they walked inside together hand in hand and the wind blew the papers off the table.

The letter made a soft landing near the boy's muddy shoes. All the alphabets fell on the floor and got jumbled up, dancing together to form new words and new stories.

Hope

The stairs were uneven, a bit like life itself. Rima climbed up gingerly, her petite frame balanced like a ballerina at every step. She was not in a rush, reaching ahead of time, twenty minutes before her train would arrive. It gave her time to settle down before she embarked on her journey to work, seven days a week, four weeks a month, twelve months a year. She would reach platform number nine and walk down to the fruit stall, next to the wooden bench. The fruit stall owner with kind eyes always smiled at her but she never smiled back at him. Smiles were rare and precious, and only for herself. She never sat on the bench either, staying on her feet made her feel alert and aware. And in some peculiar way, safe. All she did was wait for the train to come and take her away.

Rima was a pretty girl, her youth lent a fresh and natural glow to her face, the kind that needs no make-up. Her hair embraced her shoulders, a bobby pin held the bangs from falling into her dark brown eyes. She stood silently, a satchel on one shoulder, arms locked across her chest. Her solemn gaze always hovered on her worn-out sandals or ventured at best, a bit further, to the dull grey tiles of the platform. It all seemed to merge anyway. She only lifted her head when the train arrived, the only thing she looked forward to.

That particular day, she lifted her head but not for the train. As a sharp scream reached her ears, Rima was shaken out of her slumber. She thought she had heard herself. That she had unknowingly let out her carefully suppressed screams. It took her a while to realise that the sound was coming from the platform across the tracks.

An embarrassed mother was struggling to grab her child's hand. The stubborn little girl was unnervingly close to the edge of the platform and was resisting more with her screams than with her strength. Their scuffle didn't hold her attention for long though. Rima's eyes were drawn instantly to the bench next to them. She saw a young man, dressed casually in faded blue jeans and a green check shirt, his mop of curly hair falling over his forehead. He appeared as lost as her. Despite being right next to the wrestling females, he didn't even seem to notice their existence. He looked down, just as she did, right into his laptop. His backpack lay flung on the floor next to his feet. He did not lift his eyes even for a moment, as if the world would end if he did.

She couldn't stop staring at his soft and friendly face. She had an odd urge to roll her finger into the curly strands that fell onto his steadfast eyes. Her train came screeching just then, breaking her view and reverie. As she boarded the ladies' carriage she peered through the window to catch a last glimpse.

***

Home is often described by people as a place where they come back to rest after a weary day, a place to spend time with their loved ones, a place where they find their peace; a haven! A description that amused Rima.

Her house was not very big but it was beautiful in a charming way. The cream-coloured walls with large windows and a red tiled roof gave it a warm cottage like appearance. But what Rima loved most was what lay outside the house, her pretty little garden with her prized rose bushes. The only other plant that grew in her garden was the creeper on the boundary wall. As she walked towards her house, she noticed that the creepers had overgrown. She made a mental note to trim them before the neighbours complained about the mess. It was a pity they could not see the mess on the inside of the wall and she wondered if they would be equally outspoken about that too.

As Rima lifted the latch on the gate she heard him. Hesitantly she slid it off, not bothering to put it back on as she entered her hell. She spent some time inspecting her roses, taking in the red and yellow blooms. She realised she couldn't stall any longer when she heard the sound of pots and pans crashing down on the floor. Her father was home early, that was different. But he was drunk, and that was nothing new. She took a deep breath, let go of the rose bush reluctantly, and stepped into the nightmare she called her home.

****

One could make out Rima was no fashionista but the quintessential plain Jane. What did stand out though was her apparent penchant for long sleeves. No matter what the weather, Rima always wore long sleeves and long pants or skirts. She rubbed her throbbing arm gently. But today neither the floor tiles nor her sandals held her gaze for long. Her expectant eyes drifted slowly to the platform across.

There he was, lost at the same spot, on the same bench. It was a bright blue t-shirt today with the same pair of jeans. Trains would come and go, but he didn't board any of them, he just sat there cocooned on that bench. He was peering into his laptop when he suddenly broke into a smile. He started typing in short bursts as his fingers moved with the tempo of his smiles. He had a shy look on his face. Rima wondered if he was e-mailing his girlfriend. Who wouldn't fall for such a charming man! But there was more to him than his good looks. He had an aura of calm and patience and that attracted her to him even more.

Rima laughed at the childishness in her head. For once she didn't feel like she was a million years old. She tugged at her long sleeves absent-mindedly while she soaked in his existence. She wanted him to look up once, to lay his soft gaze upon her and touch her with a gentle smile. A nasty push and an impatient glare made her realise that she was blocking the door to the train that had silently crept up on her today.

****

They say routine is important to lead a calm and productive life. She wondered how her father had taken that saying and made it his own in a rather unique way. He would religiously come home drunk every single day, vent all his frustration with whatever came into his hands. A belt, a book, a chair, he wasn't finicky that way.

It was she who strayed from routine today. Instead of curling up in bed and nursing her wounds with endless tears, she sat on the parapet gazing at the moon. She peered into dreams that were yet to set in. She saw herself on the platform across the tracks, sitting next to him on his bench. Their shoulders touched as they laughed together. His laptop lay on the side, crying for attention.

Floating on her fantasy clouds she drifted back to her room. Letting herself fall on her back, with a gentle bounce of the mattress, Rima stretched her arms wide and made snow angels on her sheets, a smile on her face. Tonight her pillow was dry.

****

Rima started coming to the station even earlier than before, she wanted to be there before he arrived. She watched as he sauntered towards the bench, sometimes reading a book as he walked and at times grooving imperceptibly to his music, headphones wrapped around his ears. She wondered if he liked the same songs as she did.

She captured every movement in her memory. The way he placed his bag on the floor, making sure he zipped it up after taking out his laptop. The way his fingers lingered on the keyboard. The way he shook his curls off his forehead just to have them fall back the very next moment. She even counted the number of times he crossed and uncrossed his feet.

Rima was so lost in collecting these nuggets that she froze when he suddenly looked up, straight at her. It had been a while since she first saw him. Every day she had prayed fervently for that one look. It felt like he knew, that she was waiting. And today he chose to respond to her gaze. Their eyes met, he had a questioning look on his face and she longed to say to him, "Yes, you know me."

She did something she had never done before, something she rarely indulged in, even for herself. She gave him her beautiful smile. His face mirrored it instantly, her heart skipped a beat and almost came to a halt, as did her train.

***

She hummed a song that had been playing in her head the whole day. She tried to remember where she had heard it but was unable to. Shrugging her shoulders Rima tried to focus on more important things as she cleared up the broken pieces of glass in the kitchen.

She was considering the possibility of going across to the other platform to meet him someday. It had been two weeks now since they had smiled at each other and this morning he had even given her half a wave, one she had been too shy to respond to.

She set the chair upright and moved the table back into position, the thought of meeting him made her nervous and excited at the same time. She laughed at herself as she saw her reflection in the broken pieces of glass, and she realised she was blushing.

The music played loudly in her head, drowning her father's weary snores. She had made up her mind to at least return the waving gesture the next day. And then she let her thoughts go wild. She would walk up to him and introduce herself. Yes, that seemed right. She smiled at her bold resolve as she wiped the blood from her arms. Wondering in amazement at how it matched the colour of the roses in her garden. It almost felt like she had literally put her blood and sweat into the bloom.

***

The days were different now. The previous night didn't seem to exist any more for her. It vanished with the rising sun, with every step she took to get to platform number nine. Rima was more surprised than the fruit stall owner when she caught herself smiling back at him these days. The world suddenly seemed friendlier.

Rima took her spot next to the bench and waited patiently. She tried hard to catch his eye as he arrived but he seemed busier than ever today, headed straight to his spot, eyes downcast. His laptop held all his attention and Rima glanced at her watch.

She hoped her train would not be on time, she had to do this today. On the verge of exasperation, she calmed down as he finally looked up at her. She did a shy half wave to the young man as her heart danced joyously. The glint in his eyes acknowledged her and with a slight nod of his head, he went back to his laptop. He was oblivious to the turmoil going on inside her.

She pondered on her resolve to go across and meet him. But as her long dress played catch with the wind, exposing the cuts and bruises, her confidence lay shattered around her. No, not today. She had to let things heal first, outside and inside. How could she meet the man of her dreams in this state!

***

Rima shuddered as she saw the rose petals strewn across the garden. She knew the tornado that had done this, the same one that crossed her path every night. He took pleasure in destroying the things she loved, before moving on to destroy her. She knew she wouldn't get off as easy as the roses. He seemed to be in one of those moods when she fooled herself to believe it couldn't get any worse and somehow it did.

The door was already ajar as she warily pushed it wide open. She saw his shoes first and then the rest of him, he lay passed out on the floor of the living room. The bottle was nestled in his right hand and the carpet was soaked. The room smelt of liquor but it did not bother her one bit. His hands were lifeless and she was untouched that night.

For the first time in many days, she ate in peace. For the first time in many days, she sat in her chair by the window and listened to music. For the first time in many days, she fluttered around the house like a free bird. For the first time, she rummaged through her wardrobe to look for a sleeveless top she could wear the next morning.

That night she had a beautiful dream. Bright ribbon sashes were draped across all the benches. The platforms were strewn with roses of all colours, even prettier than the ones in her garden. Bunches of balloons flew into the skies, carefree. She was dressed in all her finery and the young man looked at her adoringly as they stood facing the full moon, hand in hand. As fireworks sparkled above them they danced in each other's arms. Had she finally escaped her hell!

***

Before climbing the steps Rima checked her reflection in the shiny door. Her yellow sleeveless top with small black polka dots looked immaculate. Her hair shone in the sunlight and her cheeks were red in anticipation. Her eyes had a sparkle and she had a skip in her step. She looked as pretty as one of her roses.

She had taken her time getting dressed today and had missed watching him arrive but it felt worth it. There he was, her knight in shining armour, on his bench, engrossed in his laptop as always. He was wearing a grey t-shirt and the usual blue jeans. She stood a bit further away than usual from her bench, she did not want him to see her yet. Rima thought she would surprise him today before he even looked up. Rushing to the walkway that joined the two platforms she wondered why stations always had to be so crowded. It didn't quite match the romantic picture she had in her head, jostling and pushing through a multitude of people to meet her hero.

Rima felt silly about how she had been dreaming like a teenager about this day. She had imagined he would gather her in his arms as she tapped on his shoulder. At times it would be a gentle peck on her cheek. Or a shy hug between the two. She tried her best to not break into a run to cross the walkway, calmly manoeuvring around the masses. Her heart was thumping as she reached the end, repeating the words in her head. "Hi, I am Rima." It was as simple as that.

A bit out of breath, she finally stepped off the staircase and saw him. She heard the whistle blow softly at first and then louder as she took a step towards him. He stood up as the train got closer. She wondered why of all the days he had decided to board the train today. Rima almost felt anger at him. And then she noticed it all. The laptop lay open on the bench. The backpack was on the floor, its contents spilling out. His face turned towards her momentarily but looked right through. The steely-eyed gaze shook her, a shiver ran down her spine. The train hurtled towards the platform as he jumped. The thunderous rumble of the train drowned her soundless screams, crushing her hopes and dreams forever.

LUCK

La Pergola, 1654

Garret Howell was not a small man by any standards, even in a kneeling position he stood tall. But today his hefty shoulders slouched and his proud head hung low from pain. The flesh from his body was torn and bones jutted out from where they weren't meant to. Strands of his long grey hair, matted with blood, fell over his fiery eyes. His body was broken but his defiance was intact. Twenty long and hard years of being a prison guard had made him strong, more mentally than physically.

He took in the macabre scene around him. Bodies were strewn all over, soldiers and prisoners sprawled over one another, contorted and disfigured inhumanly. Then he looked back at the man towering over him with a smile on his face. It was Stonehead the Red. His manic eyes were set in a large head that held no hair. Half his teeth were missing while the other half were rotting away. It made his smile look more insane than menacing. He had scabs all over his massive torso, from self -inflicted wounds.

Garret remembered having thrown him in the dungeon cell for solitary confinement. It was for Stonehead's own good or so he had thought. The others would have killed him if he had not been placed separately. His story probably scared the others so much that they wanted to finish him off in order to overcome their fears. Stonehead the Red had butchered his whole family in a fit of rage. From his old senile father to the innocent infant still suckling its mother's milk, no one was spared. He lay them all down neatly at his front door once he was done smashing their heads with the stones from his own walls. It was said that the blood flowed like a river and turned the cobbled paths red. The man never said why he did it, in fact, he never said anything ever again. Not a word escaped his mouth in all the ten years Garret had watched over him.

The act of saving him from the others may have worked but who could have saved Stonehead from himself. Good intentions don't always turn out well. The hate emanating from Stonehead the Red's eyes today told another story. One Garret would never have wanted to hear. He wondered how an act of kindness on his part could have resulted in such a darkening of another's soul. Watching the bodies of the lawmakers mingled with the lawbreakers he wondered which was which. The sight of good and evil all tangled up made him wonder if they were two separate things at all. Two faces of the same coin. As he often said, 'two sides to one story'. He didn't have the answers and he knew he wasn't going to get any.

Stonehead the Red pushed him further to the ground with his bare and calloused foot and raised a large stone menacingly above his head. Garret had no strength left to fight but that was all he had learnt to do his whole life. He curled his fist around an ornate silver dagger with a bejewelled handle, gifted by the King himself for his many years of service. It probably wouldn't even have sliced an onion but he couldn't go without holding his own till the end.

He thought as he looked straight into the eyes of death, that this place will forever be known for the fight of right against wrong, but no one will know which side was which. That's the curse of life, it needs both to keep it going. Before the dagger could even come out of the scabbard, the stone came crashing down. As it hit Garret's skull, the stone broke into small pebble-like pieces, flying all across the tavern floor, mingling with the bone, flesh, cries, and prayers of dying men.

****

La Pergola, Today

He was surrounded by loud cheering, a 'hurrah' here and a 'bravo' there. Everyone was clapping for him, a standing ovation no less. As he glided through the maze of desks and endless corridors, he felt the admiration in their eyes and the jealous pats on his back. He soaked in the ride on this wave of victory. But the cheers soon turned into screams and the weight of his success started crushing him. The wave came crashing down and he was now surrounded by a heart-breaking howl. He felt her soft hands lashing out at him in desperation. He wanted to grab those hands to comfort her but something held him back. He couldn't discern if the fear was his or hers.

Jason opened his eyes suddenly and looked frantically around him. The reticent sunshine eased him back into reality. The beer mug sat untouched on the beautiful marble table top held up by antique wrought iron legs. Glistening beads of water ran down the sides of the mug forming a little puddle near the coaster. It was threatening to engulf his iPhone, the latest model, but he paid no heed. He absent-mindedly flicked his aviators lying next to the phone, making them dance all around the table. The sweat trickled down his face and wet his collar. The limp and soaked collar looked out of place on his crisp, smart white shirt and dark blue tie. The matching pin-striped Armani blue jacket lay carelessly flung on the arm of the adjacent chair. The day was warm and sunny, perfect for a glass of beer in the outdoors and the perfect remedy for a troubled mind. Jason smiled to himself and decided to make the most of a good day.

"Would you mind if I sat next to you?"

Jason had to squint against the sun to see the man standing to his right. He was probably the same age as him, but that's where the similarity ended. For starters he was definitely more appropriately dressed for the weather in a pair of khaki shorts and a light yellow cotton t-shirt. His messy hair was reaching for his shoulders and the stubble on his chin was pretending to be a beard.

"Sure!" Although his response was in the affirmative, Jason involuntarily swept his gaze across the courtyard which had quite a few empty tables. Not one to be rude, he swiftly picked up his jacket and flung it across the back of his chair. Gesturing with his hand for the man to sit, he said pleasantly. "Be my guest."

The man had a keen eye. "I needed some shade, this patch here is the only one covered by this awesome awning. And to tell you the truth, it's kind of my favourite spot." The man dropped his weathered backpack on the ground and slunk into the chair. Kicking his tired sandals off his feet, he let out a long breath of air. His light brown eyes had a sparkle and his demeanour was relaxed.

He lacked the agitated aura that seemed to surround Jason these days.

Jason liked him instantly. "Oh yeah, I know what you mean. This is kind of my spot too. Right by the door, gets you quick service and the amount of shade is just right."

"I am in total agreement, my friend. I'm Mark by the way." He had a confident and warm handshake accompanied by a lingering smile. "Do you know how old this pub is? Some say they used to have public hangings right here, possibly this courtyard itself. It goes way back."

Jason's mood was most certainly doing a lot better now. "To tell you the truth, I do know quite a bit about this place."

Mark listened intently as Jason recounted the history of La Pergola. The tavern had been built nearly five hundred years ago by the King as a place to relax for his soldiers who guarded the jail nearby, housing some of the most notorious and psychotic criminals of the time. The same prisoners who had done the tough job of cutting through the surrounding mountains and lugging the boulders and timber to build the pub. Although the story about the public hangings was not necessarily true, there was documented information on an incident when a vengeful group of prisoners had escaped and made their way to the pub. The soldiers and prisoners brutally massacred each other in the very courtyard where they sat today.

"Not a single person was left alive, the prisoners smashed the skulls of all present in the pub at that time with whatever they could get their hands on. Bricks, stones, boulders. And the guards fought back tooth and nail." Jason knew the tale by heart. "They say the souls of the dead got as mixed up as their mortal remains."

Mark looked around the courtyard of the pub and found it hard to visualise a battle taking place in the serene surroundings he so enjoyed. The creepers on the pillars next to their table with bright yellow allamandas in full bloom, the colourful murals that gave the surroundings an artistic touch, and even the crumbling ancient boundary walls that lent an exotic primeval air to the place. Thoughts of blood and gore were impossible to imagine in the midst of this charm.

Jason pointed out an ordinary looking stone right next to their table. It had a sword carved into it, hardly visible due to the wear and tear of time.

"That stone right there was carved in honour of the prison head, Garret Howell. The pub owner likes to tell anyone who is willing to listen that Garret's soul is trapped in there. But from what I have read, it's quite likely that this stone came up nearly a decade after the guy died."

"Unless one believes in souls in limbo!" Mark laughed as he said this and Jason smiled back politely. "Quite a haunting history for such a lovely place. How do you know so much about it anyway?" Mark was intrigued by his new acquaintance.

"It's up for sale, and I am brokering it. Might make a killing here if it goes through." Jason enjoyed the cool beer trickling down his throat.

"Ah, a real estate man!" Mark said with genuine delight as Jason gave him a silent nod. "Is it just changing hands then or will they be tearing it down? Would be a shame if they renovated, although it is kind of falling apart." He took a moment's pause and said, more to himself. "I quite like this place. There's something special about it."

As they sat talking about La Pergola and its history, Mark ordered a round of beers for both of them without even having to ask. Jason felt an uncanny camaraderie with him. Was it his state of mind, was it the beer or was the sun just too hot. He surprised himself when he started pouring out his heart to Mark.

"This place is special to me too, in a rather mysterious way. My luck turned at this pub. I was struggling, nothing was moving at work, no deals coming through. It was a hot day like this one, about two years ago. I was sitting at this same table when it happened."

***

Jason had been pacing between the two pillars that ensconced his favourite table for nearly twenty minutes. Tammie wasn't sure if she should ask him for his order or just get the usual mug of beer on her own. She had gotten used to his routine for the last couple of months. Jason would stroll in, throw his crumpled jacket on one chair and himself into the other. Then would come the friendly wave and the request for a single mug of beer with a peanut bowl on the side. Over the months, this routine had stayed the same but his hair had gone from a neat crew cut to shabby locks that lay in disarray and his chin looked desperate for a shave. His shoulders were lost in the jacket that once fit him splendidly. Whatever chaos was going on inside his head had started to spill out.

The phone rang with a light trill on the table and Jason rushed for it. His frustration peaked as he saw the caller's name and he ignored the call yet again. Slumping into the chair he took Tammie out of her misery and finally ordered his beer. It was an extremely tense day for him and he needed to relax to be able to get through it. This was a make or break deal, if he was able to sell this property he would hit the jackpot. If not, he was out on the streets. He had been racking his brains all week on how to make this work.

Natalie had been amazingly patient with him but she was also a bit on edge today. Despite telling her that he needed his phone free, she had called him for the fifth time since he had come down to La Pergola. He knew she was extremely concerned for him. He also knew she would be there for him no matter which way this went. She had been with him right from the start, even when he was dirt poor and her strength had always amazed him.

But Jason was only ready to take that one call that he had been waiting for all his life. The one that would take him to the other side, to a life that would never have him wanting again. He desperately wanted to make it big, to make their future bright. The phone buzzed again and it was a message this time. He sprang up, alert.

'Mr. Brady will call in ten minutes. You better have either your final pitch ready or your bags!'

His boss was not one to mince words. Jason closed his eyes, interlocked his fingers behind his head, and reclined on the chair, the intricate wrought iron dug into his back. He pulled his head as far back as he could, trying to calm his nerves.

Stretching his legs under the table he tried to relieve the stress and let out a long breath of air. And that's when his foot struck it. He never quite figured out why he took the trouble but he bent right under, reached out with his fingers, and guided it carefully into his palm.

Jason's eyes lit up at the sight of what he had retrieved. It was a flat oval pebble of the most wondrous colours he had ever seen. Silvery grey, peppered with a musty golden brown at the edges and some shiny dark purple streaks drawn across with a fluid flair. It was roughly two inches long, one inch wide, and about half a centimetre thick. The edges were rather jagged and sharp but oddly symmetrical. Jason would have hurled it away, taking it for just any other stone but for the mysterious markings on it.

He had never seen anything like them, there was something methodical to the carvings he felt. It looked like someone had inscribed something meaningful on the stone. There were three vertical lines to the left, a few millimetres long. Followed by a series of dots in the middle, clustered extremely closely. The precision was amazing, the gap between the dots was almost the same all across. To the right of the stone after a small gap there were four wavy lines, crossing each other out at thirty - degree angles.

The best he could liken it to was a mini tablet from the Egyptian era.

He felt a sudden urge to pocket this peculiar pebble, its mysterious splendour mesmerised him. Caressing the engravings with his thumbs he slipped it into his pant pocket. And the magic began. His phone buzzed, and the name 'Brady' flashed in front of his eyes like a shooting star. For a brief moment, Jason panicked. He had been so lost in the pebble that he nearly forgot everything he had been rehearsing for the pitch. But the panic was soon replaced by uncanny confidence, a nonchalant Jason picked up his phone and let out a cheerful 'Good afternoon Mr. Brady!'.

***

Mark sat riveted as Jason shared his story. It was his beer that was puddling up the table this time. He hadn't said a single word nor asked any questions. With furrowed brows he listened intently, egging Jason on with his silent curiosity. Jason was on a roll now, he couldn't stop himself, not that he had any desire to. Sharing something he had not even revealed to Natalie made him feel lighter. He was not even bothered whether Mark believed him or not, it was good enough to let things off his chest.

"So that was the day my fortunes truly turned on their head. Yes, I got that deal. I didn't even have to put in my last pitch, they just agreed. And there was no looking back."

Jason took a long swig of his beer, his throat was parched from all the talking. Mark finally took a sip as well and kept observing him silently. Jason wasn't sure if the look in his eyes was of disbelief or amazement, possibly a mix of both. He knew what a fairytale he seemed to be spinning but he knew his truth and he just had to share it.

"I was soon being called Mr. Midas, it seemed like all I touched turned to gold. Mansions, exotic holidays, fast cars, it all just fell into my lap. I had it all!" He paused reflectively at his own words and concluded. "I still do." Unaware of how the morose and depressed tone contradicted his victorious success story, he was a bit surprised when Mark broke the pause with a 'But?'

It was Jason's turn to gesture for refills. Tammie was busy serving the family seated at the table near the boundary wall. The sun was slowly making its way home and the air was now pleasantly cool. Jason's head had started to throb, the rush of sharing a secret was probably hitting him now. Bending forward and resting his elbows on the table, he held his head in his hands and massaged his temples. He was not too keen on responding to Mark's 'but'.

"I was a winner alright, but one who had lost what was most precious to him, the love of his life. The more successful I got, the further Natalie moved away from me."

***

Her sky-blue cotton dress blew in the cool breeze, it matched her sparkly eyes. She drank the red wine delicately, savouring its taste. Strands of her dark brown hair with blonde streaks fell across her face as the wind blew from time to time. She tucked them behind her ears as she laughed at someone's joke. Jason was amazed at how Natalie had handled the success, the money, and all that came with it. She seemed to have taken to it like fish to water. Mingling at high society parties, matching the divas with her personal fashion sense, and always managing to be the centre of attraction at any gathering. He was as proud of her as she was of him.

Any mention of that unusual pebble never came up with Natalie, he didn't breathe a word of it to her. It wasn't due to fear of being considered foolish to believe in magic or luck, there was more to it. Natalie was so proud of his success, he had to claim it to be his own. He did not want to share any credit with anyone else let alone a pebble. Even though he couldn't deny something odd was at play. Jason had started keeping the stone in his pocket whenever he went out to make a business deal. He would secretly rub the markings on it during discussions and somehow things never failed to work, he never failed. It had happened way too often for it to be a coincidence anymore.

Natalie had joined in the celebrations and enjoyed every moment that came with every victory. But soon things began to change. Natalie began to change. Her appearances in public came more from pretence than real joy. She was faking it, the camaraderie with his business associates, being the life of the parties, her participation in any event associated with his work. And now the darkness had taken over their private life too.

It started as harmless arguments and disagreements. No matter where they went, how luxurious their life was or what he bought for her, nothing seemed to satisfy her. The yelling and tears were not far behind and then it came down to direct war. She hurled accusations at him and named him as the cause of her misery. The more he did to make her happy, the more she pointed fingers at him. She would accuse him of betraying her, leaving her alone, and not being there for her. She believed that she was no longer his first love, fame and fortune were his mistresses. He wondered how she could not see that all he did was for her, for them. For their perfect stable future together. The money had blinded her he felt and not him as she believed.

It was not long before Natalie started seeing a therapist and was put on medication that rarely seemed to help. It crushed him to see her, his perfect Natalie, turn into another person, a heartless stranger. As she stood there exchanging pleasantries with his boss at the cruise convention he looked at her from afar. Her gentle smile could have fooled anyone. Their eyes met across the sea of party revellers, and her cold and steely gaze pierced his heart.

***

Mark had been a patient listener all this while. Although it was hard to understand the look in his eyes, one thing was certain, there was no judgement in them. This encouraged Jason to go on with his relentless monologue.

"The more I leaned on the pebble to make things work the more it seemed Natalie was moving away from me." Jason felt it was time to wrap up his confessions. "I know how crazy this may sound, owing my success to a pebble I found right under this table. But that's how it went for me. I worked hard too, but destiny was with me all the way, things never went wrong. Except for Natalie. I have it all indeed but not the woman I love."

As Mark nodded imperceptibly Jason concluded. "I can't deny having wondered whether the stone only caused my success or did it also have a hand in destroying my relationship with her."

He laughed at himself and chugged down his beer in one go. He wasn't looking for any response from Mark yet he couldn't help but expect some reaction. Although he was relieved at having got things off his chest, he was possibly looking for some level of acceptance if not validation. Even an incredulous 'Unbelievable!' would have been acceptable to him at this point.

With downcast eyes, Mark seemed to weigh his words before he began. "So you found a pebble, that had a magical appearance. And from that moment on you tasted material success. But on the flip side, it could have possibly ruined your personal life?"

"Yes, I know, you can judge my sanity all you like. I was a desperate man grappling for any thread to hold on to for survival. But yes, that's how it has been since I found it." Jason was a bit relieved to hear Mark talk.

"And do you have the pebble right now with you? Could I see it?"

Jason shrugged his shoulders, it seemed like a fair request given the circumstances. Reaching inside his pocket he held on to it for a while, then drawing it out, he placed the pebble onto the marble table gently. He found it hard to withdraw his hand, to leave the pebble there by itself. He was afraid it might just vanish into thin air and all his luck with it. Mark leaned forward slowly, closer to the stone, refraining from picking it up or even touching it. He just studied it intently for a rather long time. Letting out a big sigh, Mark slumped back in his chair and muttered almost inaudibly.

"The day I found mine was when I got that call from Teresa."

It was Jason's turn to be speechless. He just kept staring at Mark, waiting patiently for the rest of the story. And a remarkable story it was, not very different from his.

Mark told him about the highly successful chain of cafes he ran a few years ago. He had returned home after a two-week stint in Japan, closing an important business deal with one of the leading fast food chains in the East. This was his first step in branching out internationally. He couldn't wait to share his success with Teresa, she knew how important this was for him. He looked all over for her, from the ground floor of their sprawling bungalow to the beautiful terrace overlooking the gardens. He searched from the pool and tennis courts to the beautiful woods just behind their property, her favourite place for a stroll. As his uneasiness and fear grew he called her endlessly, to a phone that had gone dead on him.

All her belongings were in the house, her car was parked in the garage but she was nowhere to be seen. Surprisingly, in all that mental chaos, he managed to notice a small scrap of paper stuck to the side of the fridge, ironically held in place with a heart-shaped magnet.

"I am leaving, it's over! That's all it said!" Mark shook his head as if he still found it hard to believe. Teresa had blocked his number, none of her friends divulged where she was, she had left him in limbo with no explanation. It had felt like a shot in the head and had completely shattered him.

"We had been together for six years and then she just left without a word." Jason saw a flash of pain on his face at the memory. Mark started frequenting La Pergola with its peaceful ambience to get away from it all. He was at the pub almost every other day, wallowing in his loneliness and that was when it happened to him. He found the pebble lying on the chair next to his. The sunlight bounced off it brilliantly, enhancing the magical colours. Mark was mesmerised and drawn to it, picking it up gently he caressed it in his palm. And the phone rang, that night, two months after she had left.

"I didn't even get time to say hello. She just said that she wanted to make things work." Mark now had that indulgent smile back on his face. "I did the same as you, I pocketed that pebble and carried it around as if my life depended on it. Whenever it seemed like something could go wrong with Teresa, I rubbed it like it was my magic lamp and things would be alright."

Jason nodded knowingly. He understood Mark's emotions completely.

"We went from strength to strength that day forward. She was my pillar and I was hers. In less than a year we were ready to get married. We're expecting our first child, due in three months." His eyes lit up at the mention of his child but Jason could see the flicker of anguish lurking beyond.

"And here's the 'but' in my story. I have since lost all of my business. It's been a slow and steady downhill process, I am nearly bankrupt. I have no clue how I will support my wife and kid."

Mark marvelled at how everyone turned away from him, except Teresa. She stayed with him through it all, she was his rock. And despite the misfortune in business, her love kept him going.

* * *

The hustle and bustle at La Pergola had died down. Old men, young girls, couples, and other strangers had lived their tales at other tables and moved on, oblivious to the exchange of the dramatic events between Jason and Mark. Both men were equally oblivious to anything around them, completely engrossed in each other's story, which now seemed like one. It was comforting for them to know that they were not alone. Things had gone right as well as wrong for both of them and they took solace in knowing that they were not losing their minds.

Jason was the first to recover from this unbelievable experience. "Wow! And to think I used to doubt myself all this time, wondering if I was crazy to believe in a pebble with magical powers!"

"Indeed!" Mark agreed. "Do you think there is some connection with the history of this place, the attack on La Pergola?"

Familiar with the pub's fabled history, Jason had already considered this possibility. "The guard had supposedly spoken about two sides to every story, the yin and yang of everything. Maybe something supernatural happened that fateful day."

The thought spooked them both a bit and they shook their heads in unison. Jason was inclined to move on from the unfortunate events from so many years ago. After all, the pebble had brought him good luck, despite his situation with Natalie, and he was keen to focus on that.

"Do you have your pebble with you right now?" He asked Mark.

Mark nodded. "Just like you, I always keep it with me. I have also never shown it to anyone for fear that it will lose its charm or powers, call it what you want."

Jason agreed. "Yeah, or even the fear of being called insane or superstitious!"

Both men smiled, their eyes reflected their trust in each other. Mark reached inside his shorts pocket and wrapped his hand around his pebble. Placing it on the table he withdrew his hand and looked away. Somehow he did not want to lay eyes on both the stones together. He felt a foreboding that he wasn't sure about but curiosity soon got the better of him.

"It looks just like yours, same markings and all."

Jason gazed at the two stones for a while and an inexplicable rush coursed through him. He spoke in measured tones. "Mark, they are not exactly the same. All the inscriptions match, except for the last lines. They criss-cross at a slightly different angle."

Mark wasn't sure what Jason was getting at but he was intrigued now. Moving the pebbles closer he observed them as well. Jason had certainly made the right observation, and he wondered if it could mean what they both were thinking.

"So while both stones seem to have some sort of power to turn our fortunes around, yours has the power of material success while mine focuses on emotional relationships?"

Jason simply nodded his head.

"And the difference in the angle of the last lines could signify which area of life we get success in!" Mark continued, more for his own benefit.

There was a heavy pause in the air as both men dived deeper into their thoughts. They looked at each other with subdued excitement.

"Do you think we could…?" Mark stuttered, unsure yet hopeful.

"Yes, it's definitely worth a shot." Jason said, staring at the pebbles nervously. He clenched and unclenched his fists hesitantly.

Both men were a bit shaken by the miracle they believed they had stumbled upon, not once but twice. It felt like the universe had intervened once again. No more words needed to be exchanged, they both knew what they wanted to do now. Hope was written all over their faces as they simultaneously pocketed each other's pebble and let out a deep sigh of relief. The thought of Natalie in his arms with a loving smile on her face beckoned Jason while Mark was already welcoming back the luxuries of life he had once known, security for his unborn child. They called out to Tammie for a celebratory round of drinks.

"I am afraid the last orders are done. We're closing down early today as the surveyors are coming around for a look." Tammie hated breaking up their party, it was good to see Jason in such high spirits for a change. She added apologetically in her defence. "We did put a notice at the entrance."

Jason and Mark couldn't have cared less, they were in a hurry to take the pebbles home and set their lives back on track. They would finally get both sides to their stories aligned in harmony, to create that much needed balance of material success and emotional well-being.

"You take care of your family Mark and let me know how it goes." Jason almost felt sad at parting with him. "And you visit us with Natalie soon." Mark was equally emotional.

Settling the bill and exchanging numbers, they set off to exchange their fortunes as well. But not before they embraced each other tightly, they felt like brothers and truly wished the best for one another.

As Tammie started clearing up a raven flew over her head and perched itself on the arch above the table. It was ragged and unclean, with feathers missing in many places and its eyes had a mean glint in them. Balanced precariously at the edge of the awning, holding on with its sharp claws, the bird pecked constantly at the frame causing some splinters to fall on her head.

"You too have a hand in bringing this place down I would say, pecking away all the time. I am tired of clearing up after you!" Tammie tried to shoo the bird away but it was stubborn and cawed menacingly back at her only to return to its diligent endeavour. The unsightly bird finally relented when she waved her apron at it roughly. As it flew away suddenly, something came loose from one of the beams and landed on the table. Tammie muttered under her breath and brushed it off with a sweep of her hand. "We could rebuild this place with all those pebbles you keep dropping here."

The shiny and smooth stone fell under the thick oleander shrub next to the table. Just behind the jagged stone with the sword carving that marked Garret Howell's bravery. It joined a small heap of similar pebbles lying partially concealed under the pink blossoms. The pebbles were silvery grey, peppered with a musty golden brown at the edges and shiny dark purple streaks. The edges were jagged and sharp but oddly symmetrical and the sun rays made them sparkle magically!

∽

FEAR

They were just sounds to begin with, but his persistence turned them into words. She realised she was being spoken to. "Please be coming Madam." The middle-aged man in the brown *khadi kurta* and bright blue jeans repeated. Rehana's eyes were glued to the 'NIKKY' written in shiny golden letters along the side seam of his pants. Madhav Singh seemed eager to please and also to show off his limited knowledge of English. Rehana was surprised at herself for not telling him that she could speak Hindi fluently. His English was rather entertaining perhaps.

But Rehana was even more surprised at her inability to move after having disembarked from the tired, dusty, and rickety bus that brought her to Derapur from Lucknow. The village around her looked even more dusty and rickety than the bus, but not tired. There was an aura of intense energy that seemed to envelope her.

Having spent innumerable days in slums with her stints at various NGOs, she had been confident that she would settle right into the village experience. She had dressed in the most basic attire she could think of, wanting to blend in. A light pink *kurta*, black *salwar*, and a matching black *dupatta*. Her hair was tied back in a casual bun which was her style anyway. She had done away with all her fake ethnic junk jewelry though. Yet she cut a rather noticeable figure amongst these people, feeling like a Christmas tree sprung in the desert. A bit like Madhav Singh's 'NIKKY'.

Ms Mamta, her project leader and her role model at the Gramin Mahila Vikas Wing had warned her. "The first time you experience it directly, is when reality hits you. But be prepared for everything. Focus on why you are going there." Rehana had nodded her head sombrely, lapping up every word that came out of her mouth. She wondered why Ms Mamta always dressed shabbily in a light cotton sari, obviously draped around in a rush. Or why her haircut looked like she had chopped off her tresses one fine morning herself without looking into the mirror. Or that her thick black-rimmed glasses always sat on her nose uselessly while her passionate eyes peered over them. The effect was that of a person devoted to a social cause and she trusted her implicitly.

But the sight of bare mud houses around her, the women in colourful attire darting curious glances at her, the scrawny men lounging under trees, and the scrawnier cows and goats sitting around equally aimlessly, did make her mind wander and also wonder. That niggling emotion at the back of her mind, was it fear? But all it took for her to focus back on her mission was a group of young children giggling at her from behind a cart laden with green leafy vegetables she had never seen before. Their joyful faces caked with a mix of snot and grime, a few toothless grins and those immensely innocent eyes did the trick to snap her out of it.

It was all surreal but it brought her right back to her senses and dispelled any doubts she had about taking the step of volunteering miles away from her comfortable nest in the city. She took pride in her decision to give back to society at the roots, to use her privileges to help those less fortunate than her. She had to share her knowledge and wisdom and bring these people up to her level. She knew things that these people didn't understand. And she knew she was one who could help remove that disparity. She knew Ms Mamta would approve of her attitude right now.

Rehana smiled at the little boy who had playfully run up to her and was tugging at her *dupatta* shyly. Arming herself with confidence and shedding any iota of fear, Rehana replied to the cheerful Madhav Singh. "Let us be going." Her little dig at his grammatical errors was most likely taken as a certification of his perfection in the language, Madhav Singh picked up her bags with a big smile on his face, one proud golden tooth glinting in the sunshine.

***

A rather large crowd had gathered around at the behest of Madhav Singh who was the main contact of the NGO in this village. There was a medley of men, women, and children of all ages. The men stood in the forefront while the women huddled in groups a bit behind them. A soft murmur went around the circle that enclosed Rehana. The little cluster was gathered right outside Sahebji's massive three-tiered mansion. The village head himself was the sole person seated comfortably on a large wooden chair kept outside the gate. He was sitting quite close to Rehana and she could feel the chill of his stone cold eyes on her.

Ms Mamta had explained in detail about the problem regarding the new girls' school that had been built recently and was lying unused. Built on a piece of land Sahebji had appropriated years ago, it had not been easy to get the construction done. But once the state minister had come into the picture, Sahebji had been completely on board with the project. His political ambitions were no secret.

The school was a bit far from the village. Not only was the distance a prohibitive factor in parents sending their girls, but so was the fact that household chores would get neglected too. It was an incomprehensible need, education at the cost of safety and housework. The boys were learning quite a bit and that was enough for the villagers.

Rehana's job was to convince these people to send their daughters to this school. To show them the power of women's education and how it could truly benefit the whole village. But she sensed a palpable distrust and unwillingness from the crowd. Feeling slightly nervous, she clenched her fists tightly and reminded herself of her just and higher cause. Fear had no place in the fight for justice. With clarity in her head, Rehana jumped right into it.

***

At first, she was the only one speaking, explaining, and persuading. She was glad she was able to speak fluent Hindi, otherwise that would have been an additional barrier to the pervading many. But slowly the villagers started opening up and putting forth their concerns and thoughts too. It was no surprise that it was the men who really spoke up and mostly not in favour. Some women seemed inclined to participate as well but furtive glances exchanged with the men sealed their mouths.

Sahebji saw no benefit in the girls learning things that would be of no use once they got married but he did not say much. His statements, far and few between, were met with grunts of approval and agreement from a gang of young sturdy men standing around him, all armed with *lathis*. They watched the crowd with great focus and alertness.

Facing this opposition made Rehana reconsider her approach. She felt the need to change her strategy to something more dramatic that would drive home the point. She needed to make an impact to get through to them all. Her eyes fell on a pretty young girl in the crowd on the opposite side from where the village head sat. Rehana walked up to her with determined strides, the villagers took a step back unable to comprehend her sudden movement.

As she came close, Rehana smiled at the girl, no older than fourteen or fifteen. Smothered in her faded red coloured *dupatta*, draped tightly over her head and shoulders, the girl returned a shy smile. Her ears, neck, and arms were bare, unlike the other village girls she had seen. But she looked beautiful with her *kohl* lined eyes which were kept demurely low but brimmed with curiosity. Rehana felt like the girl wanted to reach out to her in some way. Emboldened by this seemingly magical connection, Rehana gently pulled the girl from the crowd. She started her speech over with a new fervour. Asking the girl questions, prodding her to participate and talk, Rehana was lost in her endeavour.

A bare few sentences into her discourse, Rehana was jolted out of the blue. The young girl was pulled with brutal force from her side. A young man, barely eighteen, was dragging the girl roughly back into the crowd. His clothes were nearly rags and his body looked lean and hungry. His eyes burnt with fire from behind his long unkempt mop of matted brown hair, he glared at Rehana. Making sure the girl was well hidden behind him, he dared anyone to approach them again.

"Behave yourself. How dare you drag her like this!" Rehana was flustered and indignant. At that, the boy lost all control and gave Rehana the shock of her life. The worst that she ever had to face was the gentle chiding of her doting parents for not finishing her milk. And here she was at the receiving end of the choicest expletives being hurled at her by the young man. She was appalled to hear the boy curse, rave, and rant directly at her.

Her cheeks flushed and hands trembled as she said firmly. "But listen to me...!" With dagger eyes he hissed in a coarse and spiteful voice. "You leave my sister alone. Girls should be kept at home. Stop teaching them nonsense and ruining their lives."

Sahebji's bodyguards had now lost all composure and were totally enjoying this drama. They were laughing and sniggering while the other villagers watched in silence. Rehana was not only shocked but also felt completely humiliated. But she did not want to give up. Swallowing her pride, she tried arguing with the young man. Maybe a calmer tone would help she thought. But this only infuriated him further and he let loose another round of cringe worthy cuss words at Rehana.

Rehana felt a tug. "He is an unstable and ill-mannered boy, let him be. *Pagla hai.*" Advised a half-bent, wrinkled old woman standing behind Rehana, tapping her forehead with a crooked finger furiously and pulling Rehana's *kurta* with the other.

Some of the men now held the boy back, fearing he might let loose on the poor city girl. The women huddled closer around his sister. The village head stood up from his chair in frustration and boredom. Raising his arms in the air for silence, he called to disband the meeting for the day to avoid any further trouble. The crowds dispersed without protest, relieved to be able to go about their lives as they knew best.

Rehana felt crushed at the turn of events. They had made absolutely no progress on the matter at hand. But what made her feel worse was the way in which they all had looked at her. The young man had only hatred emanating from him. But far worse were the men, the women, the village head, and his henchmen, looking at her in pity mixed with a certain amount of disgust. Only the young girl had looked at her with warmth and empathy.

"What do they know, this illiterate lot!" Rehana thought to herself. It was the burden of intelligentsia like her to open the eyes of these people to reality.

***

Rehana shook her head in frustration as she flung her bag on her shoulder and slipped into her footwear. She had no option but to call it a day. She tried to get the arrogant village head and that rude young man out of her head.

Madhav Singh had pointed out directions to the government guest house near the new school. It would be her humble abode for the next few days. He had been called for an urgent meeting with the village head and had apologised profusely for not being able to walk her home. He was glad he had at least sent all her luggage to the guest house in the morning itself. Rehana laughed at how everyone in the village insisted on treating her like a damsel in distress. The man-woman divide was so stark out here.

Madhav's wife had packed some food for her. Some *chapattis* with fried aubergine and tangy pickle on the side. It smelled amazing and her stomach rumbled in anticipation. Giving her a tight hug of thanks Rehana realised it might not have been an appropriate gesture. But Madhav's better, and much younger, half had an amused but pleased smile on her pretty face. That cheered Rehana a bit as she set off in the direction of the new school.

Rehana intended checking it out before she crashed for the day. She was quite looking forward to kicking off her *morjaris*, digging into her novel, and gorging on the local home-cooked food. Ms Mamta had said that it is almost like love seeps into the flavour of their food. But work was work. After the fiasco, she had to achieve at least that much today. She intended sending off some reports on the condition of the school first thing the next morning. She was already making mental notes of what all she had to inspect.

***

The school was nowhere in sight. Even though she knew it wasn't close, she hadn't imagined it to be this far. Or maybe that is how it seemed with the lonely and endless road ahead of her. With night descending fast, the darkness seemed to engulf everything that came in its way. She realised that she had forgotten to take her torch out before Madhav Singh took her luggage away.

Her thoughts moved to her surroundings now and she felt a bit intimidated. There were only a few houses around, but all were empty and unlit. Even the number of houses soon started petering out slowly and they all looked more and more dilapidated as she trudged on. Some of the huts did not even have a roof, while some had their walls crumbling. There was no sign of anyone actually inhabiting these houses. They looked completely deserted.

The road itself turned from tar to dirt very soon, with stones and rocks jutting out randomly. She had to increasingly keep her eyes on the road. Rehana nearly jumped as a rat scurried across, just a few inches from her feet. She froze for a moment, waiting for any other animal that needed to cross her path. She smiled at herself for breaking into a sweat at the sight of a rat. It was lizards that were her true nemesis she reminded herself.

As she started walking again, she heard a rustling sound. But this time she knew for certain it was not that of a rat. As she became alert she could clearly hear the shuffle of feet behind her. A few more paces and she was sure of being followed. The darkness suddenly seemed to close in on her, and her heart started racing. After a few seconds of bolstering herself, she mustered the courage to turn her head around to see who it was.

Although there wasn't enough light, a quick glance was enough to recognise the angry young man who had dragged his sister away from her. His words rang in her ears, his threatening tone, the obvious anger. Fear started setting in, and her eyes darted here and there in vain. She walked faster and faster, trying her best not to break into a run. Not yet. At first, he had matched her pace, but now he seemed to be closing in.

In the distance, she noticed a building. It had to be the school, although the thought brought no relief to her tense mind. It seemed as deserted as the path she had taken so far. There were no street lights around and it was a half-moon sky covered by dark ominous clouds.

Her heartbeat grew faster, and as the clouds cleared for a fleeting moment, she could see some silhouettes near the school gate. Inching closer. She was sure there were a few men out there. As one of them lit a match to light his smoke, she could make out that they were the village head's bodyguards. She slowed a bit just to make sure, the feet behind her slowed down too. From the tone of their banter and sounds of laughter, she knew it was them. A flicker of hope burned in her. She almost smiled. All she had to do was reach them quickly or maybe just a scream would do the trick.

As she passed a small dwelling in ruins, she decided to break into a run and reach the group of men for help. But the split second decision took her more than a split-second. He was upon her even before she could comprehend what happened. He deftly pulled her behind the crumbling wall of a hut. There were wood chips, dust, and broken bricks on the floor. He pushed her down to the ground and covered her mouth with his calloused hand. Pieces of wood dug into her back and she writhed in angst. His other hand held her body down as she kicked her legs in all directions. She could hear the rip of her *kurta* as she stretched to free herself. She did not even feel the physical pain of the struggle, it was her mind that was in agony. Despite the fear coursing through her body and soul, she fought him. She kicked and lashed out. Like a ferocious trapped animal, she struggled with determination.

Rehana shut her eyes tight, she didn't want to look at those raging eyes. She didn't want herself to weaken before that smouldering glare. Despite his malnourished appearance, he was too strong for her. He was straddling on top of her now, keeping her mouth shut so tight she felt she couldn't breathe. She could feel her fear increasing and her strength decreasing.

But Rehana was not ready to give up. She had to conquer her fear. She decided to give it her all.

To look him right in those menacing eyes and give it back to him. She cleared her mind and opened her eyes. And all she saw were tears. They were streaming down his face, falling on hers. His tears mingled with her own. Too shocked to see him in this state, she let her arms and legs drop to the floor. She lay still, staring at him with questioning eyes. He relaxed his hold on her. Slowly, removing his hand from her mouth he climbed off her. Sitting on his haunches, he started sobbing softly and freely. The glare, the menace, it had all melted away.

He whispered to her. "My sister was thirteen. A lady from the city, like you, had come a few years ago. Mamta *Didi* told her to go and meet her at the guest house. She would help her learn new skills. Make her independent. Give her freedom."

Rehana wasn't sure she wanted to know more.

"On her first trip itself, they got her. She never reached the guest house."

Rehana's heart was hurting now.

"She can't sleep. Hardly eats. She doesn't talk to anyone. I can't ever let her out of my sight."

Rehana felt pain like never before.

"Nothing ever happens to them. They always get away, with everything. They are waiting for you now. They will not spare you either. And even you will not be able to do anything to them. Even Mamta *Didi* couldn't."

Rehana reached out and held his hands not knowing if she should comfort him or thank him. She could not decide what she felt more, relief or sadness. Rehana was not so sure of herself anymore. She was losing her grip on hope and confidence. Who really needed to teach whom. She now knew that there was one great leveller in life. Her eyes had been opened to the reality of fear!

Belief

I could feel it, I knew it all too well. It was like something was reaching out to my soul. My eyes closed, my nose twitched and I took in a deep breath. That's when the strong smell of the burning cumin and bay leaves hit me and I let out a great big sneeze.

"Ma, where are you?" I screamed with a raspy throat as I ran to the kitchen. In my haste, I forgot to put my slippers on and now my feet paid for it. I was hopping on the floor, trying to step away from the hot oil drops that had splattered all over angrily. I reached out and turned off the gas knob.

Mom came running in after me, her hands covering her gaping mouth. Her apologetic eyes glanced furtively at me. She tried to wriggle out of taking the blame. "Didn't I ask you to switch the gas off before I went to get the milk?"

"No. You. Did. Not!" Laying stress on each and every word made me feel rather stern.

But the smile never left my face. It was impossible to get mad at her. I tried to salvage whatever was left in the frying pan while Mom cleaned up the floor.

"Why don't you just hand over the kitchen to me, you know I am way better than you!" I teased her. Looking up at me, she smiled cheekily herself.

"If you are better than me then why are you taking cooking classes?" She wasn't one to back down.

No one understood my passion for cooking as well as she did. In fact, she was the one who had submitted my application for professional cooking classes.

"Endless hard work for me now. Classes will be every Sunday morning, on top of college. Look how dedicated I am. And all of this, just to give my Mom a delicious meal!" I was totally enjoying the nonsensical banter.

And like any ridiculously proud mother, she responded. "You don't need classes. You are like the Master of Kitchen."

"It's Masterchef Ma. We have been watching that show for years now and you still can't get the name right." I said, shaking my head dramatically.

Mom might have had some trouble with her English but little did I care. She was way ahead of her time; my rock, my partner in crime. And we both goofed up on exotic cuisines together. As we both laughed, wiping our hands on Mom's apron, I noticed Dad's looming shadow at the kitchen door. I poked Mom at the waist and we quickly smothered our giggles. The clock ticked silently in our heads, waiting for the impending boom.

He stared at me for a full thirty minutes. Or maybe it was just thirty seconds, but it felt like an eternity. He finally managed to blurt out. "Cooking classes!" His mouth was still open for another fifteen minutes so I wasn't sure if it was a question that I was supposed to answer or if he was going to follow it up with his usual sarcasm. But it was his eyes that baffled me. I couldn't quite make out what was dripping from them in greater quantity - surprise, anger, or contempt.

"God knows what's next!" He said, as his mouth finally closed and his eyes popped back into their sockets. "I am so tired of your nonsense. People your age are married and settled down. And you, what are you doing with your life?" His eyes were still ablaze but his shoulders had slumped.

"Don't trouble my baby!" Mom shot back from behind me.

But Dad was in his mood. "First, it was interior decoration, now this. I have been saying, get married, settle down, nobody listens to me!"

"Sweety, you go wash up. I will quickly make some pasta for you, just like that Gordon Ramji." Mom carried on too, Dad may well have been invisible to her.

"Ramsay Ma, Ramsay!" I laughed as I watched Dad retreat quietly from the battlefront.

Mom just had to open her mouth to make me laugh and Dad had to open his to make me cry. I must say, it was a pretty good parental balance.

***

Finally, the first Sunday arrived. I was almost as excited as Cherry. No one could ever be as excited as Cherry. Especially when someone was getting ready to leave the house. It somehow inevitably meant that they were going to take her out for a walk. And right now she knew it was me. If she could have, she would have certainly helped me pick out my clothes so that I would take her out sooner. And she seemed to be keen on pink today. Grabbing my new t-shirt between her sharp teeth, she started running around me in circles till I was the one who got dizzy.

"Sorry honey, I will be stepping out alone today." I said to her lovingly, as I gently pried my precious top out of her sharp fangs. But in dog speak this probably meant, 'We will leave in two seconds' because she seemed even more excited and was running all over the room now.

I quickly wore my things and stepped into the living room to ask Dad for some money. Before I stepped into the danger zone I heard his phone ring. It was Big Sis. Or rather, the perfect daughter, as my Dad made sure to point out every now and then, just in case I had forgotten.

"Look at your sister. She works with an MNC. And at the same time manages a beautiful house, a wonderful husband, and such a well-behaved three year old."

I remembered these lines better than my name, age, or address. The journey to Dad was wrought with more hurdles. Along the hallway, on the wall, there was a sugary sweet family photo with the impeccable daughter in her Dad's arms and the reluctant black sheep being pulled by Mom to be part of the picture. Even in the photo, his eyes seemed to glare at me. I decided to take a detour and sneak out as fast as I could. Luckily I found a crumpled hundred rupee note in my jeans pocket. This would have to do for now. I was in no mood to hear yet another analysis of where I had gone wrong in life, what Dad had done to deserve me, and the endless list of expectations that I had not fulfilled. I kickstarted my scooty with an extra amount of energy today and zoomed off to the land of aromas.

****

If ever the phrase 'all eyes were on me' rang true, it was today. My hands were a bit shaky as I kept my helmet on a desk near the door. I ran my fingers through the hair around my shoulders to untangle the knots caused by the wind. It was also an action I normally performed to soothe my jittery nerves.

I walked down the aisle, more nervous than a bride-to-be. They looked at me as I walked to the front of the class. I knew I was late but I didn't think I deserved that much attention. Not many could have withstood the looks that I got from this mix of young, chatty, self-assured girls & a few excited and nosy old aunties. I wondered if I would fit in with this lot.

Shaking the unnerving thoughts out of my curls, I decided to focus my gaze on the matronly looking lady dressed in a smart blue cotton sari at the head of the classroom. She was standing erect next to a whiteboard, looking into some papers in her hand; she was probably the only one who hadn't stared at me yet. As I coughed politely, the papers finally lost their charm and she obliged me with a quick glance.

With a smile that had fake written all over it, she said. "Yes, can I help you?"

"Sorry, I am late. I am here for the class."

"You are here for the cooking class?" She enquired, her eyebrows almost touching the ceiling.

Before I could instinctively point out that she hadn't had her eyebrows plucked in months, thankfully Mrs Gupta's impatience stopped me from goofing up on my first day.

"OK, please sit."

Finding the first empty chair in the second row, to the extreme right, I jumped in and slouched down to avoid being noticed too much. I seemed to have succeeded in my endeavour. The girl next to me did not give me a single glance and was focusing very earnestly on what Mrs Gupta had to say. I myself was drawn to how immaculately dressed she was, in a pretty light brown polka dot top and a smart black skirt.

"Hey, your top and skirt look lovely." I opened my mouth in a lame attempt to get friendly.

I probably didn't say it as softly as intended. The whole class seemed to have heard me and I soon heard hushed giggles from rows one and three. For a moment I naively wondered if I had messed up my English like my Mom. At least polka-dot girl was a bit polite and returned my compliment.

"Your pink top is quite nice too. And the skinny jeans really suit you."

At that the rest of the class burst out laughing. I shifted my chair a bit away from polka dot girl, as the mean streak in her *kohl* lined eyes bore right into me.

***

On reaching home I saw Mom waiting at the door, impatience written all over her face. Tapping her right foot furiously as I parked the scooty, she could wait no more. Mom grabbed my hand as I stepped onto the porch and pulled me hurriedly towards my room. Now I got that she was as excited as I was about these classes but she was taking her eagerness to another level.

As we passed the couch in the living room, right opposite my Dad's favourite rocking chair, the rocking came to an abrupt halt. A sharp, 'Stop!' echoed in the slightly large hall. Dad lowered the book he was reading on his lap slowly and determinedly. He looked straight at me and said as softly as he could. "Sit down, we need to talk." I now understood Mom's eagerness to take me inside to the safety of my room.

While Mom obediently did his bidding on my behalf, I continued standing behind the sofa and found myself tugging at my hair yet again.

"Sharmaji had called. He wants to fix a day for....!" Dad started.

But before he could finish, I stopped him in his tracks. I even dared to hold my hand up, a first in our many quarrels. In a rather curt tone I said to him, without meeting his eyes. "I had a good day. And I have many assignments to hand in at college next week. I am not in the mood to talk about marriage right now and mess it up."

I had to ruin Mom's plans of a nice long chat and walked off to my room all alone to show that I meant business. Dad fumed as I slammed the door behind me while Mom sat sadly on the sofa twiddling her thumbs.

***

Another Sunday came by, and another class. By now I had learnt to keep my distance not only from Ms Polka Dot but pretty much most of the people in the class. I focussed on what I did best. Cooking. Also, that way I didn't have Mrs Gupta breathing down my neck constantly.

This week, cool desserts were on the menu. I decided to keep my cool too and stay out of Polka Dot's hair. But unfortunately, Mrs Gupta wanted some entertainment today.

"You will be teaming up with Puja, go to her table." She gave me the marching orders.

As I walked despondently over, I saw myself fascinated, yet again, by how well she was dressed. She looked like a princess in her peachy, knee-length dress, with little pink flowers on it. She had really good taste in clothes and I wished I had even half of that. But since that first polka top disaster, I had never gone beyond secretly admiring her dress sense. Trying to ensure that we kept the peace I said to her cheerily. "I am pretty good with sweet stuff, this should be fun."

Puja smiled and said nothing. And like a fool, I insisted on taking that as a friendly gesture. Just as we dropped spoonfuls of sugar into the flour, a young man entered the room and started talking to Mrs Gupta. He was the cutest guy I had ever seen. A tight olive green t-shirt that showed off his rippling muscles, hair gelled stylishly. He looked like he had just stepped off a flight from Greece.

I couldn't keep my eyes off him. And Ms Polka Dot couldn't keep hers off me. I was lost in my world when I felt her deep breath in my ear and heard her say. "That's Mrs Gupta's son. What a hunk, right?"

And her eyes, I couldn't quite make out what was dripping from them in greater quantity - surprise, anger, or contempt. I wondered if this was Puja or my Dad in disguise!

She wasn't looking for a verbal response, she was just waiting to see my ears and cheeks go red. And her rant continued. "Is he your type. And I do wonder, are YOU his type!"

There wasn't a single question in there, just sarcasm through and through. Even though she was almost tripping into my ear, rest assured she wasn't whispering. She made it a point to say it out loud. And again, the sniggering started. The glances, the murmurs, like silent stings.

I dropped an additional spoon of sugar into the bowl. Something had to make up for the bitterness.

***

Cherry nearly knocked the teacup out of my hands as she playfully jumped onto my bed.

"Get off the bed you naughty monster." Mom looked rather angry. "Don't you dare lick the snacks." And that was the extent of her anger. As she gently put Cherry on the floor, she slipped down some treats for her as well. We had made this our new Friday ritual. Mom would make the tea and I would treat her to some new dish I had learnt in class. We talked non-stop on no topic in particular. I felt like I was in paradise. Everything was perfect. And in walked Satan himself!

This time Mom nearly dropped her teacup when Dad stomped into the room. Flinging his phone on my bed, he stood there glaring at me silently. Mom started to clear up the signs of our revelry but that seemed to anger Dad even more.

"Stop doing that!" He roared. He never really raised his voice at Mom so I must be in some serious trouble I thought. Bringing his laser focus back on me he continued. "What all I have to hear because of you! Sharmaji's niece goes to that damn cooking class too."

I tried to work out in my head how my going to the same cooking class as Sharmaji's niece was such a big crime.

"She told him what happened with that boy the other day. What is wrong with you? How shameless can you be? Haven't I suffered enough?" His voice cracked as he said these words.

I wanted to open my mouth but I knew there was no point. There was nothing I could say that would make any difference. The verdict had long been passed on me.

"You are not going to those classes anymore!" He declared, in control once again.

I just stared at my tea in defeat while Cherry whined innocently for some more treats, blissfully unaware of life. Putting the whole plate on the floor, Mom took our unfinished cups and walked out of the room.

****

And the Sundays just wouldn't stop showing up, again and again! The week's theme was Italian.

I could see the delicious pasta, the spaghetti, the gnocchi, floating in front of my eyes. My mouth was watering already.

"I am sure you would have won." Mom sighed. But I didn't want to upset Dad. I figured I had done enough of that my whole life.

Mrs Gupta has announced a contest for today. And I was all prepared to beat that pesky Puja with my special pasta recipe. I did wish I could have just beaten her up literally too I must admit.

Mom didn't have to say anything, the way she looked at me was enough. "OK, I'll go!" I agreed, more for my benefit than hers. Although being sneaky was not who I was, I had to somehow get past Dad without him knowing. Just this once, for the sake of my excellent culinary skills. But he stayed glued to his book right in front of the main door, gently swaying on his chair. And then as always, it was Mom to the rescue, she gave me a knowing wink and embarked on her surreptitious plan.

"Can you go get some onions, we have run out?" It was an order, not a request.

Dad let out a big irritable sigh and gripped his book tighter. "Do you need it right now?"

Mom nodded silently. The lesser you said with Dad the better it was. He would pounce at any extra syllables that came out of your mouth and turn them around and fire them right back at you. Dad shot a glance at me hoping to rope me into this but I just covered my face in as many books as I could, the bigger the better.

Mom's time-tested strategy worked. Having nothing in hand to counter, Dad relented, stood up, and got the grocery bag. He seemed in deep thought as he started to leave. He was walking painfully slow. I observed him carefully as he walked to the door. I knew that time was running out but suppressed the urge to check my watch. I took a deep breath and started counting in reverse under my breath. "Ten, nine, eight, seven...!" A little drama never hurt.

As I reached two, he stopped in his tracks. Mom and I looked at each other. He fumbled for something in his pocket. Seeming satisfied that he was well armed with enough cash, without looking back, he left for mission onion.

I sprang from the sofa right to the door.

"Are you going like this?" Mom started with her silly questions.

As I hurriedly settled on my scooty I said. "I look so hot, you could cook on me right now Mom!"

Mom laughed and shouted. "Show that polka dot girl who is Big Boss!"

"It's 'who's the boss' Mom!" I laughed.

"What?" She said, straining her ears over the roaring of the scooty.

"Never mind. Love you." I replied as I sped off.

High on my mom's spirits, I was ready to take on the world, starting with Puja.

***

It was close to evening. As I silently glided and parked at the porch, I could sense the doom and gloom in the air. Dad was sitting in his rocking chair. But there was no rocking, just a static heavy rock. His focus was on the door like a cheetah, waiting to pounce on his prey.

And he started the moment I entered. "Look at yourself. How you dress. How you behave. Do you realise how old you are? What have you done in life?"

As he said those hurtful words the day's class flashed through my head. And tears welled up in my eyes. Cherry came and stood between my legs, with her tail between hers.

He wasn't done. "Disgraceful! Shameful! Why were you even born!

I just stood there listening silently, letting the tears flow down my cheeks.

Mom rushed to me and held my hands. "My baby! You are a strong person. You are smart, confident, and independent. Don't listen to your Dad."

I looked into her kind eyes. "Dad just said nearly the same words that Mrs Gupta said to me today. After humiliating me, she said that she could not have a person like me in her class. And told me to leave."

"I don't care what she said Ma. She means nothing to me. What others say doesn't matter at all. I can take it."

"But what your own people say does matter and is very hard to handle!" I said that looking straight at my father this time. But his eyes were on the floor, burning the tiles now after having charred my heart.

I went to bed without eating the special dinner Mom had made in anticipation of my non-existent Italian conquest.

****

The next week went by in silence. Dad stayed away from me and we refused to speak to each other. Even Mom's positivity couldn't raise the shroud of darkness that had settled upon us. I felt worse for her than I did for myself and I couldn't do this to her. As Sunday approached I decided to break the ice. Dad had started reading in his room since my Italian Sunday fiasco. Sitting in a rather uncomfortable plastic chair by the window, he didn't seem impressed with whatever he was reading. His eyes wandered.

"You can talk to Sharma Uncle. I am OK with it." I said softly.

Suddenly his book became exceedingly absorbing and Dad couldn't take his eyes off the pages now. He didn't say a word. Mom stopped folding the clothes on the bed next to his chair. Her face fell. She knew what I was going through.

"Don't be silly. No need to make hasty decisions. We love you no matter what." She implored, more to Dad than me.

"The 'we' doesn't sound right Mom." I couldn't keep my voice from cracking. As Dad let the book fall into his lap and closed his eyes, I saw a lone tear roll down his cheek.

＊

And the day after Saturday dawned upon us yet again. I sat on the sofa in my shabby t-shirt and track pants surfing cookery channels. Mom had been trying to convince me to go for the classes but that ship had sailed. She sat next to me with a glum face, stroking Cherry on her lap. Just then Dad walked out of his bedroom, dressed smartly in a blue check shirt and black trousers. Cherry was the first to perk up her ears and let out a low yelp. Even she was surprised to see him like that.

It was Mom's turn next, in a guarded tone she asked. "Where are you off to?"

Dad maintained his serious air. He looked straight at me. "Get ready."

Now Mom asked cautiously. "Is Sharmaji coming, should I change too?"

Dad ignored her again and gave me an impatient look. "We need to go, now!"

For once, Cherry finally understood it wasn't always about taking her for a walk. She stayed put in Mom's lap. And Mom stroked her furiously, not knowing what else to do.

As for me, I hardly ever questioned my Dad and now was certainly not the time to be experimental. I quickly changed into my jeans, spraying the crumpled t-shirt from last night with dollops of deodorant. I glided into my flip-flops and grabbed my bag. I refused to make any mistakes at my end.

Without a word, we sat in Dad's car. He drove without looking at me. And I didn't dare ask him anything. It didn't take me long to figure out that he was driving in the direction of the cooking class but when he parked right in front of the building, it still managed to surprise me. I was eager to skip two steps at a time but controlled myself and stayed a step behind all the way to the classroom.

The session had already begun and there was flour and salt in the air. As we stepped through the door together, the ladies turned around and looked at us with amazement and amusement. Mrs Gupta, in a stiff starched white cotton sari today, walked towards us slowly, cautiously. Not sure what she was in for. I must say, I was in the same boat as her, equally nervous and confused.

She maintained a safe distance and stopped at least a couple of tables away from us. Her right hand rested gently on a saucepan, just in case she needed to exercise some self-defence. The rest of the class looked on in anticipation. They all seemed to be hoping to move on from cooking classes to drama classes or even martial arts. Ms Polka Dot tried to sneak into a chair with the best view. Only the popcorn was missing.

Before Mrs Gupta could exercise her vocal cords, my dad cleared his throat and took lead.

"We have been trying your recipes at home and I absolutely loved them. You are a brilliant teacher."

All Mrs Gupta could come up with was a mumble and a pinch of a smile.

He continued, putting a loving arm around my shoulders.

"So here I am to join the classes, with my son. And I am very proud of him!"

TRUST

Sonya stood in the middle of the room, hands on her hips, head tilted to the left. Her hair was loosely tied up in a bun threatening to cascade down her slim shoulders. Her eyes were glued to the peach coloured wall. It was the only wall with no windows or doors in the living room. It was a canvas for her memories, framed for eternity.

Pictures cosied up in old wooden frames. Making sandcastles with her brothers at the beach. A dazzling victory stance at the mountain peak from a lone spontaneous trek. At a picnic with her mother, before the cancer made it impossible for her to even step out of bed. Dressed as a Minion for a Halloween party with her best friend Becky. Making silly faces with Roy at their first New Years' party together three years ago. The only people you can show your crazy side to are the ones you have known a bit too long.

Looking at fragments of her beautiful life spread across the wall, a smile crept across her face as she felt complete bliss. There were still five more boxes to unpack but she already felt settled. Everything was perfect, well almost. The sooner she could get her night shift moved to a saner day routine, the happier she would be. "There is always room for more happiness." Becky always said.

As she bent to take out a picture of her gang at work, Roy grabbed her from behind and planted a gentle kiss on her neck.

"Why did you have to move out here? I hate the idea of not seeing you every day."

Sonya turned around and put her arms around his neck. "We have to make do with weekends then, for now."

"But that's not enough baby!" His pretend whining was so adorable.

"We discussed this. It makes sense to live here given my odd work hours. Once you get that transfer and move to this side of town, we can just live together, day in and day out!" She admonished him lovingly as she traced a finger down his bare torso, slowing down at every bump his rippling muscles formed.

Roy gave a hearty laugh, pried the frame from her hands, and threw it back in the box. "Yeah, with your night shifts, daytime is all that is left for us."

Sonya made a glum face with pouting lips. Although Roy had been extremely understanding about the move, she herself was not entirely happy about them not meeting as often anymore. The guilt was weighing on her mind.

Roy pulled her to the sofa and drew her onto his lap. "Well, at least the location is not bad. I do need to come this side of town for a lot of things, so I can make it over pretty often I guess."

Heaving a sigh of relief, Sonya hugged Roy tight. "Let's look at the bright side. And make the most of this daylight that we have, in the moment, right now."

Roy stroked her ear and said playfully. "Right now?"

Sonya let out a laugh and jumped off him. "Yup, let's make the most of it and empty all the boxes before my shift begins."

＊＊＊

Leaning wearily against her door, Sonya waved to Roy as he pulled out of the driveway. It had been a week now, the house had started to feel 'lived in'. The hardest part was not seeing enough of Roy. But she kept her fingers crossed for the day he would move in with her.

"I am working on it, anytime now darling." She clung to those words. Sometimes her need for Roy scared her as much as it brought her joy.

Her gaze swept across her new neighbourhood. Charming dwellings with their whitewashed walls, red-tiled roofs, and pretty little gardens in the front. Organised in neat parallel rows, the houses were small and very close to each other, a bit too close for comfort as far as Sonya was concerned. Not quite the one to mingle, she wondered how long it would take her to even get to know people, let alone make friends. This whole week had flown past in just unpacking and getting her bearings.

Sonya spotted her closest next-door neighbour just as she was about to shut her door. An enchanting middle-aged lady stood there, looking straight into Sonya's eyes, unabashedly. Long dark hair let loose, she had a mysterious and friendly twinkle in her eyes, quite like the shiny accessories and bright clothes she seemed rather fond of. They had seen each other a few times earlier and each time opened up in silent smiles.

The woman gave a brief wave. Sonya thought she would walk up and say hello to her. It was high time and she did look quite approachable. The exotic artefacts at her doorstep that she had been admiring all these days would make a nice topic to start the conversation with. But as she stepped down her front porch, a young woman rushed towards her, blocking her way.

"Hi, I am Mona, I live right behind you, a bit to the left, number twenty five. Sorry to stop you like this but I just wanted to come by and say hello. Do let me know if you need anything."

Intriguing is what came to Sonya's mind as she sized up Mona. She was quite fashionable, dressed in black hot pants and a shimmering yellow tank top. Sonya couldn't help but admire her neighbour's stylish appearance. With matching block heels and a glitzy handbag, she looked all set for a party.

"Hey, thanks. I was just stepping out to say hello to the people around, get to know them a bit." Sonya nodded towards her silent neighbour who was standing calmly at her door watching them.

"That's sweet but I have some advice. Be a bit careful with your mysterious neighbour." Mona said a bit nervously, lowering her voice. She signalled to the next-door house with a quick wink of the eye, arched eyebrows, a generous tilt of the head, and a rather obviously accusing thumb. Mona's lack of subtleness was not limited to her dressing sense Sonya gathered.

Although taken aback she prodded a bit more out of curiosity. 'To each his own' was more her motto but it would be wise to know who you lived with in the neighbourhood.

"We all stay away from Maya. Some strange things go on in that house. Chantings, odd music, fragrances, and smoke at odd hours. Although it's kind of primitive to say so, I am pretty sure it's got to do with black magic."

Sonya took it all with a pinch of salt and indulged Mona for a bit. She did not want to be judgemental about anyone. She thought she would meet Maya and decide for herself.

Maybe over the weekend, it was nearly time to get ready for her night shift now. As Mona left in a rush for her party, Sonya looked back at her neighbour who had gone back indoors and Sonya desperately hoped she had not heard any of the words that Mona had said. She suddenly saw Maya appear at the kitchen window, waiting to look her way, Sonya smiled as she caught her eye. This time it was met with a disconcerting emotionless stare and a smile that never reached the rest of her face.

* * *

The mat under her feet, with intricate abstract patterns and bright splashes of red, green and yellow, mesmerised her. The whirling silver streaks were almost hypnotic. The big brass knocker shaped like a unicorn had made a surprisingly loud sound when she rapped it at the door. Sonya knocked again, gentler this time.

She often caught herself wondering about Maya these days. They had exchanged a few pleasantries by now. She appeared soft-spoken, shy, and reserved but had a strong presence. It was not just the way she dressed, her being exuded an energy that always made Sonya feel a sense of peace and calm. But then there was the other side that unsettled her a bit. At times Sonya would catch Maya peering into her house. When she and Roy were together. Could she be one of those nosy neighbours!

Sonya decided to go by her gut feel. Maya seemed dependable and harmless, with the added advantage of always being around and Sonya needed help right now. As Maya opened the door after quite a few knocks, a waft of incense enveloped Sonya. It was a sweet smell but a bit too strong for her to handle.

"Sorry, I was meditating." Maya said in her heavy yet unidentifiable accent. Her dark long tresses engulfed her round face. Oddly not a single piece of metal adorned her body today. The bareness was oddly attractive. Even her dress was unusual, a shapeless flowing satin white robe, that swept the floor as she moved back from the door gesturing at Sonya to step in. She almost looked angelic despite the dark black, gleaming, witch like eyes.

Peering into the unfamiliar darkness inside the house, Sonya decided to stay where she was. It somehow made her feel safer out there. "Hi, I didn't mean to disturb you but it was rather urgent." Sonya said apologetically, genuinely feeling guilty now. "Could you give these keys to Roy, please? He seems to have misplaced his and he will be coming home tonight while I am gone for work."

Sonya held her hand out with the keys dangling uncertainly in the air as Maya stood there in silence, peering into her soul. She cleared her throat not knowing what to do next and her eyes shifted under the relentless gaze.

"Of course dear!" Maya said unconvincingly and fell silent yet again, the keys still dangling in front of her, waiting to be taken.

"I hope that's okay, I am not imposing, am I?" Sonya just wanted to pocket the keys and turn away now, unsure if taking such favours was worth it.

Maya's eyes flickered momentarily and she rose out of her stupor. Responding normally this time she assured Sonya. "No, not at all. If neighbours won't help, who will." Her eyes were friendly now but there was still a tinge of tension in the air. "If you don't mind my asking, is Roy your boyfriend or fiancé?"

"Boyfriend!" Sonya had no clue where this was going. The conversation was making her even more anxious now and she giggled like a nervous teen and blabbered on. "Hoping it's going to be fiancé very soon!" She even brought up two crossed fingers up to her face to embarrass herself further.

But Maya was in a world of her own. "He reminds me of someone I used to know." She looked lost in her memories.

Sonya tried to sound light-hearted as she nervously racked her brain looking for escape routes. "Probably one of those common faces, the boy next door." Sonya kicked her brain from the inside.

Finally taking the keys from Sonya's hand, Maya ended the ordeal. "I hope you two are happy, it's nice to see two people in love." Her eyes did not reflect her words. Sonya hid behind the safety of her sunglasses and with a quick 'Thanks' she rushed to her car. Mona's words clouded her mind.

***

"It's rather odd Becky." Sonya whispered into the phone as she did the dishes. Roy had snoozed off after helping clear the table. "I have been here two months now and things seem to be unsettling rather than settling."

Becky had grown accustomed to these regular complaints. She mostly just hummed and hawed in response. She understood that all Sonya needed was venting, not solutions.

"Remember I told you about that picture of me and Roy lying on the floor when I got home last week? Some very odd things have happened since. I find pieces of furniture out of place. My clothes lying in odd places. Books pulled out from the shelf."

"Could you just be confused about where you put things?"

"I even smell odd fragrances at times. You know I get a headache with any kind of strong smell. I can't be making that up. It's driving me a bit crazy." Sonya went on.

"Why don't you talk to Roy about it?"

Sonya shrugged her shoulders. "You know him. He doesn't believe in that kind of stuff. If I were to even mention Maya or that I feel odd about her, he will get mad at me. As it is he doesn't like her much, he says she stares at him whenever he drops by."

Sonya cut the call as she heard Roy stir in bed. She couldn't deny the odd happenings around the house no matter how lightly Becky treated them. Maya's unpredictable and odd behaviour was no comfort either. At times she would come towards her as if approaching her for a chat but would hesitate, mumble and turn right back without making any conversation.

She was always doing these odd chants and prayers. Burning things at midnight in her backyard, performing odd rituals. Sonya felt like she could see Maya peering into the house at all times and it didn't feel like harmless neighbourly curiosity. But what beat it all was the fragrant smell that came constantly from her house, Sonya just couldn't stand it.

Despite all these thoughts, she couldn't imagine Maya being involved in whatever was happening in her house. And nothing bad had happened anyway, just some things out of place. Sonya went back to her wall of memories for peace of mind. Pushing the slightly tilted photo frame with the New Year click into place, she went back to daydreaming about when Roy would move in with her.

***

The street light streamed in weakly through the sheer curtains. The darkness was overwhelming. It did throw enough light on the turquoise blue tank top that Sonya held in her hands though. The little pink cherries on it were bright and alive. "It goes so well with my khaki shorts." Mused Sonya.

Roy had quite the knack for shopping and that too for women's clothes. Not an attribute found in too many boyfriends. He had bought this one for her from his trip to Hawaii. She seldom took it out, in order to make it last forever. She loved seeing that desirous glint in his eyes whenever she wore it, so it only came out of the closet when Roy was around.

But after the incident this morning, she felt like throwing it away in the garbage. She had wanted to wear it for Roy before he left. She had attacked the neatly set cupboards and chest of drawers like a tornado, leaving clothes hanging out, lying on the floor, and strewn on the bed in her attempt to find it. Her frustration had raised her temper in equal proportion.

"It's happening again. Where the hell is it?"

Roy briefly tore his eyes from his book, lounging on the rocking chair in the bedroom corner by the window. "What are you up to?"

"I can't find it. The top you got for me last summer."

"That's one sexy top, wear it for me baby." His eyes returned to the book.

Sonya's glare bounced off him unnoticed. "Are you even listening to me? I can't find it. It's vanished!"

"Vanished? What's that supposed to mean?" Roy was finally curious. Placing the book on his lap he looked at the room with wide-open eyes, taking in the mess that surrounded him.

Sonya realised she had let herself slip. Roy would be furious to know her thoughts on the matter but there was a limit to self-control. Things didn't just disappear into thin air. And she was in no mood to attribute it to a figment of her imagination. She had to do something about this. She could feel Roy's eyes fixed on her as she marched to the front door. She knew he had followed her and was now leaning against the main door watching her as she stomped determinedly to Maya's house. It was like someone had taken over her mind and body. Every action just flowed.

She glided past the sound of her name being called out, oblivious to Mona who was approaching her as fast as she could in her shiny black stilettos, balancing precariously on the cobbled stones. Even her loud clothes couldn't distract Sonya from her mission. The unicorn rapped furiously at Maya's door. And even before the door was half ajar, Sonya's dam burst.

"Where is it? Where are all my things going? Who's moving stuff around my house?"

The look of sadness on Maya's face was the last thing Sonya was expecting. Anger, shock, possibly even fear was what she was ready to deal with. But Maya made no attempt at responding or reacting and this shook Sonya even more. Placing one hand aggressively on the door frame, she moved in closer to Maya who smelt of a curious combination of jasmine and ashes. Her other hand shook as she pointed at Maya accusingly, her finger, a mere inch away from the heart.

"Why do I always find you looking into my house? Why are things going wrong?"

Maya placed her hand gently on top of Sonya's, still silent. Not knowing what else to say and not entirely aware of herself, Sonya curled her hand into a fist and let it drop by her side. She too joined in the embarrassing silence. Broken soon by a meek and hesitant 'Sonya' from behind.

Mona was standing sheepishly right in the middle of the two houses as if trying to stay safe in a no man's zone. She had a folded piece of clothing in her hands, turquoise blue in colour.

"I think this top flew over the fence and landed in my backyard. I'm sorry, I meant to return it earlier but...!"

With whatever self-respect she could garner, Sonya slipped her hand out from under Maya's. Tracing her steps back to her house, lifting the top wordlessly from Mona's outstretched hands, she walked right past Roy to the bedroom. Shutting the door behind her, she sat silently in the chair.

The whole day she kept rocking back and forth, with the top in one hand and Roy's book in the other. She was wondering if now she, instead of Maya, would become the talk of the neighbourhood. Maybe Mona was already warning some other resident to stay away from the crazy new neighbour. But she had no doubt on how Roy felt about her disgraceful performance. He had not asked her to open the door even once. All she heard of him was the slam of the front door and the car speeding off, away from her.

***

"You don't look so good Sonya." Her boss looked genuinely concerned. Sonya had a terrible headache from the moment she came to her desk and had been sitting for the last fifteen minutes with her head in her hands. She felt it would explode.

She just nodded back to him without looking up. There was too much on her mind besides the headache. While leaving for work that evening, Sonya had bumped into Maya. They had not faced each other for nearly two weeks after that awful incident. Neither did she have the courage to apologise nor the intention. But Maya had surprisingly carried on as if nothing had happened. She was quick with her smiles even if she didn't get any response from Sonya.

That evening, running late for work, Sonya was fishing frantically for the car keys in her bag when she almost knocked the platter out of Maya's hands as she walked right into her. A platter full of odd-sized incense sticks and candles. As the fragrance made her reel back she wondered if she was hallucinating or there really were a couple of doll-like figurines buried under a mound of flowers on the plate.

Maya had looked a bit surprised, a rare emotion betrayed. The whole blend of incense and flowers had entered not just Sonya's nose but deep into her soul. It made her head spin and she felt like throwing up. Mumbling an incoherent apology, she left Maya behind to pick up the flowers strewn on the path, making sure there was no more eye contact.

Sonya leaned back into her chair with her eyes closed as she pondered on her life. She could blame Maya all she wanted but she couldn't deny that the real trigger for her despondent state was the massive argument she and Roy had a few days earlier.

"The branch transfer looks very unlikely, I might miss a promotion." He refused to meet her eyes when he said that.

Sonya looked him square in the face. "But we discussed this, you had said you would figure this out."

Roy flung the book he had been flipping through absent-mindedly. It fell on top of the other two that had been lying under the shelf for a week now. Sonya had stopped putting things back in place just as much as she had stopped trying to find the reasons.

"Things change, damn it!" He screamed at her, directly this time.

Sonya fell further into her abyss as she remembered their exchange. She couldn't concentrate on work and kept fighting back the tears. Roy's change of mind, Maya's strange behaviour, and the inexplicable happenings in her house. The madness filled her heart and head, as did Mona's words. Sonya decided she would talk to Roy about this after all. He needed to know about Maya.

＊

Her head throbbed to the rhythm of the beats of the song playing on the radio. Sonya eased slowly into the driveway and parked the car. Thankfully there had been enough people to cover for her tonight as she took off early. She sat inside the car for a while fiddling with nothing in particular. Switching the radio off, she wished she could somehow switch off the torrent of a million thoughts churning inside her head.

She couldn't wait any more to get things off her chest and share them with Roy. It was probably better that way instead of burying it all inside. She decided she would call him before crashing for the night and ask him to come on Friday instead of the usual Saturday. They could take a call on what to do that weekend itself.

"I will leave this house and move back in with Roy, even if I have to quit my job." You have to give up things for the people you love. If not Roy, it had to be her. They had to work together on this. Maybe things do change as Roy had said and life was about handling change.

At last, relieved at having taken a decision, she got out of the car and walked home. As she wearily opened the door, her feet froze and stuck to the floor. She stood gaping at the sight in front of her. It was dark as the curtains were fully drawn. But the soft glow of scented candles of different shapes and sizes burning all over the living room gave it a mellow soothing hue. But it wasn't the fragrance of the candles that made her nauseous.

A beautiful woman was standing at the bookshelf, browsing through a book. She was wearing bright red lacy underwear and Sonya's favourite t-shirt, the one that had belonged to her mother. Her heart broke into a million pieces as she watched Mona let the book drop carelessly from her hands when Roy came strolling from the bedroom and grabbed her roughly from behind. He kissed her neck and shoulders passionately. She ran her fingers through his hair as he pushed her to the peach-coloured wall, pushing Sonya's framed memories askew.

They were oblivious to Sonya, completely engrossed in each other. Kissing, caressing. Sonya stifled her gasp. Stumbling backwards, she stepped out the door and quietly shut it behind her. She lowered herself onto the porch steps, her legs buckling. Even her tears were too shocked to make an appearance. She jumped ever so slightly as a pair of arms, decked in golden bangles, enveloped her in a comforting hug. Maya's eyes were sad and sympathetic. With a gentle knowing squeeze, she took her hand and led Sonya away.

Misery

The door slammed shut, it made the windows rattle but the screws on the hinges took the hit valiantly. She felt like doing it again, taking it all out on the door. Somehow she resisted, opened it again, and looked at the two confused human beings on the other side. The children held each other's fingers loosely, unsure if they needed the support, peering up at her with a confused look in their eyes.

Disha managed to flash a weak smile at them and a quick peck on the cheek was enough to clear the confusion. Children don't need explanations or reasons, a little bit of love is enough for them. They looked at each other, giggled, and ran off to catch their school bus, not in the least bit interested in knowing why their mother had slammed the door at them. She wished she could be as blissfully unaware of life as they were.

As often happens with frustration, it wasn't about them. The previous night's screaming and shouting with Arun was still ringing in her ears and all she wanted was to be alone. As she curled up in bed she pondered on the years gone by, it wasn't the first time they had fought in their ten years of a mostly happy married life. But the altercation had an ominous feel to it this time around. She was seriously worried about their relationship.

He had left earlier than usual for work today, having showered and shaved even before her alarm went off. He had shut the same door gently behind him as she fumbled to pack his lunch. Disha reached out and ran her fingers soothingly over the box lying on the bedside table, tracing all the edges. She felt as unwanted as the rolls inside.

She tossed and turned, wishing she had drawn the curtains before she hit the bed but it was too late now. The sunshine poured in like a sparkling stream insisting on keeping her awake. Disha needed to get out of the house to stop the moping. She rolled off the bed and walked straight to the door. Her daily dose of a walk by the lake was the only thing that cheered her up these days.

She looked at her crumpled grey top and saggy black track bottoms for a brief moment and then proceeded to slip on her shoes. She did take the trouble to pat her hair down in the mirror on the adjacent wall, but it didn't help much. She looked every inch the mess that she was. And she didn't care. She did make sure that she shut the door softly behind her this time, an apology lurking at the corner of her eyes.

***

The tingling fresh morning air and smiling, energetic faces made her feel good. She was glad she had pushed herself to step out. Not only did the walk keep her in shape physically it also lifted her spirits. At least there were some people in this world who were happy she thought. As she finished her three rounds of brisk walking, she headed straight to the bench at the far end of the lake. The trees were dense here and the crowds sparse. The quiet was only broken by the intermittent chirping and buzzing of unseen birds and insects.

But the bench was not the cynosure of Disha's eyes. It was the person sitting on it, as always, every single day. A frail old woman who exuded an aura of easy elegance. Her hair was all white with a few black strands fighting hard to make their long lost presence felt. The light blue sari was draped around her immaculately, not a single pleat out of place. She wore no jewelry, not even a single golden bangle that ladies her age invariably had on, more as a part of their history rather than a fashion accessory.

Disha liked to think of her as the unknown companion at the lake whose quiet presence reassured her in some way. She had never seen her walking, only perched still like a statue on the bench, gazing at nothing in particular. There was an odd mix of despair and calm about her. They never exchanged names, not knowing each other up close and personal somehow made it easier for them to unburden themselves. Taking turns naturally, no advice, no comments, no reactions, they simply provided a metaphoric shoulder for each other to lean on. The bench may well have been a couch.

With a half smile, Disha sat down and matched the old woman's listless gaze. They never greeted each other, not even a simple hello. Their eyes hardly ever met. At most a knowing nod was all they exchanged.

"Business is getting worse. Just a great big loss on all fronts." Disha paused as a young jogger cut across their view, chasing elusive dreams. "It's getting to both of us. We fought like dogs last night. For no reason whatsoever, it's just stress!" She analysed and concluded solemnly. She didn't dream these days, awake or asleep. Keeping up with reality was hard enough.

Nodding her head knowingly the old woman spoke up after a few seconds of silence. "My daughter is having a terribly tough time, all because of me. The doctor said yesterday that I need surgery urgently." She turned her neck ever so slightly to watch a carefree little girl plucking flowers from a shrub nearby. "It will cost a lot of money. I don't know where she will get it from. It's not like money grows on trees."

They had an unspoken pact, to not ask questions, to not force the other to reveal any more than their heart truly wanted to. It was a kinship in which they let each other be what they needed to be in the moment. As they bonded with purging hearts, the joggers, walkers, children and dogs, even the butterflies and birds, all went about their business.

***

Her eyes kept darting to the kids' bedroom door but she couldn't stop herself from shouting. She knew they could hear them squabbling. Even Arun matched her today, decibel for decibel, despite being the soft-spoken one. She couldn't even recall how it started, why it started, or what the trigger was.

"You think I don't care about the kids!" He had an incredulous look on his face, hurt in his eyes.

She knew this was the time to hold herself back but it just poured out of her incessantly. "What kind of life are we providing them? What about their future?"

"And it's my fault, am I not trying to save the damn business?" It went on and on, going in circles and tangents and other geometric patterns.

Till a few months back they would make sure the kids were in bed before they discussed anything but now they hardly even noticed their presence. The children did not have to be told to go to their rooms, they sensed it even before Disha saw it coming and beat a retreat well in advance.

Her eyes fell on the photo frames on the shelves. People are always smiling in pictures she thought, and here they couldn't even manage to fake it. She missed those smiles. Picking up one that had all four of them from their last holiday, she tried hard to try and remember where it was taken and when, to no avail. Not that it mattered. What mattered was that they were sitting together on the grass, each holding up a cone of ice cream, exaggerated ear to ear grins pasted on their faces while Arun took the selfie. She walked up to him and placed the reminder of a cherished moment in his hand. They held it together and drowned themselves in their memories for a split second. Grasping each other's hands to stay afloat, they came back to the surface, with grim faces, set to face an even grimmer reality, together.

***

A deep frown adorned her forehead and her eyes squeezed shut tightly. She tried to conjure up her children's smiling faces, that was one thing that always amazed her. No matter what the situation, they always found a reason to smile. And their smiles always gave her a ray of hope, something to hold on to. But she gave up and let out a sigh, her imagination seemed to have abandoned her.

"It's impacting the kids now, they can see it. He is under so much stress." Disha started tugging at a thread that had come loose on her shirt. "We will have to pull the kids out of this school. As it is the driver, maid, have let them go, one by one...!" Her thoughts lingered unfinished.

Resting her feet on the bench she drew her legs close to her chest, a shield to her heart.

Taking her turn, the old lady said. "It's just getting more and more painful. I can't bear it but I try." She caressed the veins jutting out from the thin skin that enveloped her hands. "How will my daughter do this! She has sold off the jewelry I had saved for her wedding. First, she slogged for her father's illness and now for me." She cursed the diseased blood flowing in her veins pointlessly.

"I am trying my best to support him." Disha assured herself.

"I am doing all that I can." The old lady responded in an echo.

Leaves floated down as the wind darted through the branches of the trees. Maybe things would have been different if the leaves had the strength to hold on firmly Disha contemplated, stretching her hands impulsively to save them from falling to the ground.

For a fleeting moment, Disha felt an uncanny desire to take the old lady's small hand in hers. She had always felt that their words, no matter how vague and incomplete, known only to themselves, ended up in a bond of their own. They drifted away into the air holding hands, bolstering each other, escaping reality.

The clouds turned dark as the gentle breeze turned into a gale, making the trees sway dangerously over their heads. Their deep sighs merged in the gust of wind as they contemplated their individual complicated lives, together.

***

She couldn't take her eyes off his crooked tie but he was oblivious to it. Her hands itched to fix it but she held back. Bigger things were in need of fixing.

Arun had held his hand up wearily when Disha handed him his lunch. "There's a meeting with the lawyers today, I will most likely eat out." This was the only sentence he had said to her in the last two days. She had kept her calm and stayed silent too. She found it fascinating how sometimes words can do wonders and sometimes it is the silence that tides you by. Knowing what works when is the tricky part.

She had gone from spiteful tirades to desperate whining, calm discussions, and more. Now it was time to give silence a chance to work its magic. She was ready to do anything it took to help them get through these tough times. Disha hugged Arun as he left to meet the lawyers again. He had been a mess the previous night. He had broken down, cried, and sobbed his heart out. This was the first time he had truly let her feel the gravity of the situation and how helpless he felt. The lawyers had thrown in the towel. There seemed to be no easy way out. If he wanted to save his company too many sacrifices would have to be made. Too many difficult decisions to be taken. The business she had watched him nurture for years, his dream, she now watched it falling apart, taking him down with it. He was a hard worker and an honest man. Luck had simply turned against him.

She rummaged frantically through her cupboards and drawers to see if she could find anything else to sell. As she sat with empty hands at the dresser, she looked at herself in the mirror. She fingered the only piece of jewelry left on her body, the thin gold chain that Arun had gifted to her when he had proposed. She had not taken it off in ten years. The memory made her eyes sparkle like Arun's had that day. And now all she saw in his eyes was despair. She longed for her image to hold her tight. To assure her that things would get better. But her reflection was drowning in a deeper silence than herself.

***

The sun was scorching, Disha had a hard time completing her rounds. Her quick-dry red top was soaking wet. She rushed to the cool shade of the Gulmohar trees but the sun was not the only reason for her exhaustion. The mental had spilled to the physical. Spotting the old lady at the bench gave her some solace.

Disha had often wondered why the lady was always there before her and always left after. Was it by design, did she sit there the whole day, did she talk to anyone else? The questions arose in her mind and took root right there. She never even felt the desire to ask. They both knew they could be completely selfish with each other, only venting their grief and finding their peace of mind. That was all they needed from each other. Focusing on yourself can sometimes be a more fulfilling endeavour.

"I have sent the children to their grandparents. We are eating into our savings." Disha's lips quivered as she continued. "Nothing has helped. He has to shut down his branch office. Slowly everything will go. I am scared he might do something drastic."

She knew Arun was a tough man, but life could be equally relentless. The possibilities frightened her. She wasn't sure if talking about it would make the possibility go away or make it more real.

"She screamed at me last night. My daughter has never done that before. Her frustration is taking over her now." Tears clouded her already misty eyes, as the old lady began. "I know she didn't mean it. But it is hard for her, people say things behind her back. She just took it out on me."

Disha could hear the heartbreak in the woman's voice, she could feel the yearning to make it easier for her child. She felt it herself every day for her own children.

"I don't know what she is doing to organise the money. I should probably just die." The words came out with a disturbing aura of calmness and determination.

The thought of death sent a shiver down their spines. Drawing strength from each other's presence they tried to look beyond their own despair. Even managing a smile at a bunch of colorful balloons that rushed up to the sky. The small boy who had let go of them on purpose was jumping up and down and clapping his hands in joy as the blue, red, and yellow dots merged with the skies. There was possibly some good in letting go but how could you do it with the ones who you loved so dearly, the price of freedom seemed excruciatingly high.

***

Just making it to the bench was a torturous crawl. She didn't even bother to attempt one round. It seemed like years had passed since she had been to the lake. Disha could see some new faces rushing past her with energetic and purposeful strides. The trees looked bare, the flowers had no colours and even the noisy crickets seemed to be meditating. Had things changed or was her mind playing tricks on her. The only reassuring constant was her silent companion who still sat at the bench, gazing at the unknown with unwavering dedication.

In a tired and broken voice Disha managed to begin. "I can't believe it's only been three weeks. It feels like the whole world has changed. It was crazy. The branch office shut down, the whole staff lost their jobs. This was after months of no salaries."

The old lady's silence meant it was still her turn. And Disha did have more to get off her chest. The weight of every single word made her voice heavier, she had to force them out.

"The branch manager couldn't take the sacking and committed suicide. My husband's name was in the suicide note. The police arrested him."

Disha swallowed a couple of times and her voice started cracking now. She was finding it hard being the only one confiding. She wanted the old lady to take her turn so that she wouldn't have to live her experience yet again. But she went on in the face of stony silence.

"It's been hard on the kids. They haven't seen him for so long but it's best for them. Not that I know what is wrong or right anymore."

A young couple with a toddler between them walked past, holding her hands on both sides, teaching her how to walk. Disha watched the parents' joy at every step their child took. She shuddered at her own children's uncertain future.

"He's out on bail now. On sedatives, severe depression the doctor says. I can't bear to see my Arun like this."

As the tears rolled down her cheeks Disha felt her companion's gaze on her. She lifted her head and looked into a pair of eyes that had run dry. Eyes that wanted to ask a thousand questions but needed no answers.

"My daughter died three weeks ago. Her suicide note named her boss Arun as the reason for her death."

For the first time, the two women looked into each other's eyes, their wailing words trapped inside them forever, never to be shared again.

Love

It had been a while since Varun had inhaled that familiar fresh air. Three years to be precise. Life at college had been engaging in more ways than one. Although he had been sucked into a life full of projects, papers, and parties, Varun always had *Nanu* on his mind, especially when he read a good book, or possibly any book at all. At eighteen it had felt alright to postpone visits to his grandparents, life lay ahead for him. And he had wrongly assumed it did so for his *Nanu* as well.

His Mom put an arm around his shoulder as she joined him under the majestic cedar. The house was perched at a vantage point on the hilltop. On one side there was a road that led to the hustle-bustle of the rest of the town while the other side overlooked the sheer drop into a valley full of coniferous trees that glistened with dew, silence being the only sound one could hear. The mansion itself was a beautiful sight, blending in aesthetically with its surroundings despite its large size. The walls merged into the thicket of trees that surrounded the house on all sides, along with a garden that slowly unfolded beyond the doors into blossoms of all colours.

Nanu had been a very successful businessman, the richest man in town. But those were not the riches that had made Varun cherish his grandfather. It was their shared love of books. His fond remembrance of Thakur Vir Dayal Kashyap was interrupted by a gentle call. "Come and eat children." Varun had heard this call so many times during his literary escapades with *Nanu*. His grandmother always had impeccable timing, just when they would be at a part of the book that had both of them engrossed, *Nani* would call out for her food platter. Varun and *Nanu* would shout out in response. "But we love the book platter more!" It had been their private war cry, one that always had them in splits every time *Nani* got a plate of goodies for them. He devoured the food much the same way he did the books, with energy, gusto, and delight. The war cry was just one of the many ways to bond with his *Nanu*.

But there was no war cry today, just moist eyes. The three of them did a silent group hug and sat down to eat some food, none noticing what they picked up or put in their mouth; all lost in their memories of the much-loved man.

***

It had started with his first visit to his grandparents who lived in the mountains. The journey from his busy city in the flat and straightforward plains was a tough one. The five-hour train ride provided dull views of barren brown land which was followed by a three-hour car drive surrounded by innumerable trees, a solid contrast. As beautiful as the views were from the car, the journey was full of twists and turns, going higher and higher made him sweat with an unfamiliar queasy feeling.

He had travelled alone by train for the first time, now that he was a wise ten year old. His grandparents came to pick him up at the station. He was seeing them after four years, with not too many memories and he was unsure what to expect.

Nani embraced him with a bear hug, the rolls of fat sat comfortably on her and so did her double chins. Her face was set to break into a loving smile the moment she laid eyes on Varun. *Nanu* stood at a distance, a large and imposing figure. A thickset moustache and a square jaw gave him a stern look that went against his sparkling, warm eyes. His *pahadi* hat sat tilted on his head, looking as uncomfortable as *Nanu* himself. He grunted inaudibly at first and then managed to mumble a 'welcome'. *Nanu* was quiet all the way home, while *Nani* held his hand in a tight grip, not saying much herself. They all seemed to be sizing each other up, making Varun wonder how he would spend a whole month with them when the car ride itself was proving to be a challenge.

Initial interactions were awkward, he didn't know them, and they didn't know him. But *Nani* was always ready with delicious snacks and that was fun for the first few days. He soon tired of her food and desired to discover the mysterious man that was his *Nanu*. He was around most of the evenings but seemed far away even when with him. They never knew what to say to each other. Until one fine day, Varun strolled into the large hall right at the back of the sprawling house that had eight bedrooms, a dining hall, two sitting areas, one courtyard, multiple *verandas*, and a lavish living room. It was no wonder it took him three days to discover it.

Varun felt no less than a pirate who had stumbled upon unexpected buried treasure; he had walked into a library. His jaw dropped as he saw the rows and rows of books, of all shapes, sizes, and colours. His mother used to tease him that they would host his wedding at a library and for all one knew, he would marry a librarian. It was no secret, Varun was a certified bookworm. And right now he was in book heaven.

He nearly jumped out of his skin when he suddenly heard a loud bang. The hammer started beating with a disciplined rhythm, almost like percussions for a song. Peering from behind a shelf he spotted *Nanu* fixing a wooden plank that was falling off the wall, with at least twenty books slanting precariously, ready to ski down the shelf and onto the floor from a height of six feet. Just when Varun thought his *Nanu* would fall along with the avalanche of books, he saw him give one fierce slam with the hammer and set the plank right back in place. When *Nanu* spotted Varun staring at him in admiration, for the very first time, *Nanu* bestowed upon him a beaming and warm-hearted smile. Varun smiled back with the same magnanimity, he was beyond joy at learning about this treasure his *Nanu* owned.

"You also love books?" Varun didn't feel so shy anymore.

Nanu replied, a bit sheepishly, with a question of his own. "Which one is your favourite?"

Varun started talking about all the books he loved and his *Nanu* listened patiently. A bond was forged forever.

The next morning *Nanu* was at Varun's bedside when he awoke. In his hands were the books Varun had enquired about the previous evening in their endless chat. Varun had been curious about all the books that were there in the library and *Nanu* had promised to reveal them to him in his own unique way. Varun could ask about one book in the evening and *Nanu* would bring it to him the next morning, give him a summary of the story, and then Varun would have to read it for the next three days. They would then sit together on the fourth day to discuss everything about the book. And then they would do the same with another one. Varun had never been more fond of a routine in his life. And this way, when his grandfather was away looking after his lumber business, he would not get too bored. He enjoyed *Nani's* cooking and the way she fussed over him but books were his comfort food.

By the end of summer, the two had become inseparable, always leaving a trail of books behind them wherever they went. *Nanu* started taking time out from work to be with his grandson whenever he could. Neither noticed when *Nani* would come and go, silently watching the two bond from afar, a loving and indulgent smile on her face.

***

Six weeks went by like a breeze. Varun and *Nanu* took walks during the day in the garden laden with rhododendrons, red, yellow, and orange. The chilly nights were spent in front of a warm fire cuddled up together, surrounded by books and a delicious bowl of steaming hot soup on the side. *Nani* always scolded them for reading in poor light under a lamp but they refused to go indoors. There was something enchanting about reading outside in the dark under a sky full of stars.

Sometimes *Nanu* would take Varun along to work or when he went into town to meet people. He would introduce Varun to everyone proudly, always making it a point to let people know how fond he was of books. During these visits, Varun learnt how respected his grandfather was. He had been the son of a poor carpenter and had taught himself skills and the ways of the world. He had built a magnificent business empire in timber that spanned at least five cities. He had earned the respect of everyone he knew, even the elders called him '*Thakurji*'. He was a self-made man and Varun's hero.

And Varun himself loved being the centre of his hero's life. *Nanu* would make him read out loud from the books. But the best thing was that *Nanu* never corrected him or pointed out mistakes, he let Varun be. He always said that a man had to learn from his mistakes, then only would he be truly self-made. And Varun nodded in agreement, as he did for everything else *Nanu* said.

He did not know as much about his grandmother but he loved the stories he heard from the house help. His favourite was the one their driver had told him once on the way home after dropping *Nanu* at the warehouse. *Kaka* was an excellent storyteller with a tendency to exaggerate, but then it is those juicy details that make any story that much more interesting. It turned out, as per *Kaka*, *Nani* had run away with *Nanu* in the middle of the night on a horse! They got married against her parents' wishes. Although Varun could not quite imagine his grandparents riding a horse, what amused him, even more, was that his quiet *Nani* had been quite the rebel. Nor could he ever understand why anyone would not have accepted his amazing *Nanu* as a husband for her.

At times *Nani* would join in their private meetings. "He will be a famous orator when he grows up, the way he reads his books." *Nanu* said one day with unmistakable pride in his eyes as Varun narrated a passage from a classic. *Nani* chimed in. "Why not a famous writer?"

He knew she meant no harm and was only trying to be a part of their fun but Varun did not like anyone disagreeing with or doubting what his *Nanu* said. "I will be what *Nanu* says."

Not realising the emotion in the boy's tone *Nani* continued. "A writer is closer to books than an orator." Varun had no clue what got into him but he couldn't stop himself either. "What do you know about books? I don't even like this soup you made."

He felt ashamed the moment the words came out of his mouth, but he did not know how to set it right. Childish anger and guilt filled his heart. Hanging his head low, he picked up a book and hid behind it, unwilling to see the pain in *Nani's* eyes. Expecting a scolding from *Nanu*, he was surprised when he heard him say in a calm and jovial voice. "Well, he could be both!"

And as soon as *Nani* had left, he put his arm around Varun. "Your *Nani* loves you. Do not make the knowledge of books be the standard you judge people by." Varun shrunk with shame but took it on the chin like a man. He resolved to improve his behaviour. But his *Nanu* soon had him feeling much better as he spouted a saying. "Truth shall prevail!" He always had Varun in splits whenever he would rattle off a famous quote, completely out of context.

Despite Varun's genuine attempts to mend things, *Nani* now mostly kept away when he was with *Nanu*. There was no decrease in her warmth and love but she preferred to leave the two alone with their common love and interests. Maybe she felt she didn't fit in, which was true after all in his eyes. He wanted to be fair but he was only a child, one who adored his grandfather above anything else.

***

Most of the following summers went by the same as the first. Varun devoured more and more books as he grew older. And *Nani* lurked around with her unconditional love and platters of food. There was one summer though when *Nanu* had to travel for work. Varun was in a big dilemma, he knew he would get bored at home. The fresh mountain air always did him good and he loved being at his grandparents' house. *Nani* would be nice to have around and *Kaka* would regale him with absurd and entertaining stories. But it wouldn't be the same without *Nanu* and he refused to go.

He moped around the house, watched the city life through his window, brought new books from the library, and missed his *Nanu*.

"But *Nani* will be there, you know how much she loves you." Mom said as she handed him a bowl of popcorn. It was movie night and Varun had chosen Harry Potter. He loved watching movies based on books.

"I need the right company not love." he replied obstinately. "She can't even read a book."

This made his Mom fly into a rage but Varun stood fast to his decision. A decision that upset both his mother and grandmother.

"I know Ma but this isn't right, he can very well spend quality time with you too." He heard his Mom complaining to *Nani* on the phone. He peeked from behind the door unable to change his mind despite knowing he had hurt them both.

"Why don't you ever say anything? I am so proud of you, he should be too, just because of *Baba* he treats you like this." Varun felt ashamed at what his Mom had said and decided he would make it up to *Nani* on his next visit.

But grandmothers do not hold grudges and children will be children. Henceforth *Nanu* made sure he was around for all vacations and time flew by between the three of them, grandfather and grandson in arms and grandmother at arm's length.

*****

Varun spent a week with his grandparents before he left for college. His visits had become shorter over the years but never lacking in love, joy, and fun. His taste did change in books and he had lesser in common on that front with *Nanu* than before but the shared love for books kept the bond strong. They spent most of their time in the library, *Nanu* working on building his mammoth study table, Varun reading out to him despite the noise, meandering between the shelves. *Nani* would drift in and out with her goodies every once in a while, a radiant smile ever present on her face. It was a bittersweet holiday, with Varun looking forward to starting a new life while trying to spend as much quality time as he could with his grandparents. His life would soon be full of new experiences while his grandparents would cling harder to old memories.

The bond stayed strong even though infrequent. Varun sent letters to *Nanu* from college and also the occasional book. Over a phone call, they would then discuss the books once *Nanu* had read them. Although still active at work, his grandfather had toned down his responsibilities, spending more time at home. In his letters, he would tell Varun how he was doing carpentry work around the house, like his own father. He seemed content and at peace. Varun in return would give lengthy accounts of his college life. He made sure he gave all details even if *Nanu* was unlikely to understand half of them. There was a deep desire to connect at both ends no matter what the content.

"*Thakurji*, did he ask about me?" *Nani* would often ask *Nanu*. Her yearning for her grandsons' love never diminished. "Yes, of course, Devyani." *Thakurji* would reply as confidently as he could, his eyes betraying the truth. She had made her peace with her husband getting the larger share of their grandsons' love and respect, mustering a smile she would nod silently in return.

They both waited for Varun to return, in every phone call, in every letter he would promise.

"Next holidays for sure." Varun had embarked upon the life of the young. Busy, hectic, full of excitement and opportunities. At times it would be a project that kept him busy, at times an internship, and at times just a simple preference to go holidaying with his gang to the happening beaches instead of languishing in the solitude of the hills.

His grandparents didn't mind, no matter how much they missed him. Varun loved how *Nanu* always encouraged him to focus on himself and make the most of life and the opportunities in front of him. Even *Nani* never pressed him to make his visit a priority. Varun's Mom tried her best to take time out from her busy schedule to be with them instead of him but it never quite measured up. *Nani* always teased her that she could never replace Varun as she did not share his passionate love for books. And so life went on between letters, books and phone calls and the now routine question, "*Thakurji*, did he ask about me?"

***

Only Varun knew how much he regretted not having come earlier, not having had the chance to say goodbye to *Nanu*, and not having read one last book with him. It was dark now and the cold wind bit into him along with the guilt.

"I guess I'll hit the bed now." Varun hadn't said much the whole day and the two women also had pretty much just nodded their heads absent-mindedly all through dinner without a word. He hugged his Mom and *Nani* and headed inside. Something felt incomplete as he headed to his room, the one he always slept in during summer breaks. It had not been used since he left for college. He felt the urge to visit the library, the place where his adventures with *Nanu* had begun. He had to pay homage to him there, nothing could be more befitting.

Varun's heart lit up with warm memories as he entered the hall lined with shelves. The books took him back to his childhood. Running his finger along the book spines, he walked around the room, taking in the familiar sights and smells. The Adventures of Tom Sawyer, Malgudi Days, Lord Of the Flies, To Kill A Mocking Bird. The pristine collection of Amar Chitra Kathas. The numerous autobiographies. He felt like a sailor on a rough sea, going up and down the waves of hardbound memories. He travelled across every nook and corner of the library before heading to the grand mahogany table that his grandfather had built himself. He would spend hours sitting there. As he sat on *Nanu's* chair Varun's eyes fall on some papers strewn on the tabletop.

Engrossed in the scribbles on the sheets, he did not realise when his mother and grandmother entered the library until Mom placed her hand on his shoulder. He stood up suddenly and in his excitement knocked a few papers off the table. His eyes shone bright, as he randomly grasped a few sheets and waved them in front of his Mom.

"Look Mom, it seems *Nanu* was writing a book. Maybe a memoir or something. The pages are filled with our stories, all we did during those summer holidays." He was smiling like a ten year old and bubbling with excitement. His Mom smiled back at him weakly.

The joy starting dissolving into grief and Varun was now in tears. "He loved me so much, he wrote a book about us. He even named it The Book Platter, it was our private joke." Varun fumbled on the desk to look for the paper with the title on it. His grandmother reached out hurriedly as if to gather the papers in her arms, seemingly to take them away from him and Varun lost his temper as he had once before.

"Don't touch his things, *Nanu* was writing this for me. Stay out of it!" Once again he cringed inside as he let loose on his dear *Nani* as he had years ago. "We were a team, *Nanu* and I. You don't belong with us. You never did."

As his *Nani* stepped back, his Mom stepped forward and held him tight. She met his blazing eyes with a look that was at once stern yet loving.

"Your *Nanu* did love you a lot Varun, but he did not even know how to read or write."

She let her words sink in. Varun's jaw dropped and he stared blankly at his mother. *Nani* looked beseechingly at her daughter while drawing her shawl tightly around her shoulders, a desperate attempt to keep things under covers in some way.

"Your *Nani* did all the paperwork for him."

"But... the stories, the books, and those letters...!" Varun left the sentence hanging in the air as realisation dawned.

He looked at his grandmother with eyes full of sorrow and unsaid apologies. It took him a while to gather himself and walk up to his grandmother who had shrunk into her sadness. He held her tight till she finally relaxed and they hugged each other like never before. Varun tried to give his grandmother the love and respect he had held back all those years unknowingly in that one long hug.

Together they collected all the papers and set them in order, neatly on the table. None realised when dusk turned to dawn as Varun heard the real stories, the ones kept hidden from him for so long. The sacrifices his *Nani* had made to nurture the relationship he had with his *Nanu*.

With the first chirp of rising birds, Varun walked across *Nanu's* table to finally keep his promise of making amends with his grandmother. His Mom smiled as Varun put his arm around *Nani* with pride and held up the page he had been looking for. He announced, to the grand audience of countless books that surrounded them. "The Book Platter, by Devyani Dayal Kashyap, my *Nani*!"

And the books witnessed with joyous anticipation, a new bond being formed, delighted in the knowledge that they would yet again provide an unshakable foundation to another lifelong relationship.

～～

Passion

⸺⸺◦✦◦⸺⸺

The colours were mesmerising, multiple hues of orange and red covering the entire sky. She loved those colours, the colours of life she called them. And she loved watching sunsets. He wished she could be here with him. Holding hands and watching the sun vanish behind the mountain tops, it was on their list of things to do when together, that endless list.

He decided to message her. It was hard to stay away for too long. Although he had decided he wouldn't do it these five days, on holiday with his old college gang. He had hoped to get busy with them and not be tempted to connect with her.

But he couldn't help it, he missed her too much. She was always on his mind, as he was on hers. Her message from last night was stuck in his head.

"I wake up with thoughts of you & go to bed with you on my mind. And then dream of you when asleep. Talk about 24x7!"

He smiled at her cheesy lines. He loved them so much.

He noticed Sid watching him with a frown on his face. Taking his hands out of his pockets he rubbed his hands together, not necessarily for warmth.

"This isn't good buddy, your obsession with her."

He ignored Sid and kept watching the sunset.

"You have to stop it. You know it's going nowhere. Move on."

He still didn't respond but he knew Sid was right. But then, he loved her too much. He also knew it was never meant to be. Her marriage and his emotional instability, it had always been a crazy combination. The hiding, the secrecy, the stress of a forbidden relationship. It was too complicated right from the start. But they had connected like soulmates from day one. It was different. It was special, the bond they had. How could they have ignored that. How could he let go!

She had messaged before leaving.

"Don't ever let go of me."

He had promised her, written it at least twenty times.

"We will be together, forever."

***

They were all planning to go for a swim. The thought was refreshing but he was feeling restless. He sneaked out into the hotel gardens to message her. He just had to stay connected to feel alive.

"Missing you so much. Wish we could have done a holiday together at least once, just you and me."

Her response was immediate.

"Sweety, where have you been? What took you so long? When you are with friends you forget me."

He smiled. She always acted like a drama queen and he just adored her when she did that.

"Lol. Cut the drama. It was so pretty on the hilltop. The sun, the sky, the colours, just wanted you here with me."

She responded with a sad smiley.

"Someday. I always keep my fingers crossed, no matter what!"

He heard Sid calling out to him from the window. He quickly typed to her.

"Going for a swim honey. You had said I should take a break from you once in a while. Am trying. But it's hard. Will ping soon."

She responded instantly.

"You can do it baby, it's best for us."

***

He played with his food. Everyone was talking around him.

He tried to participate in the conversation but somehow everything just reminded him of her. He remembered how they both used to laugh about acting like romantic love-struck teenagers. But it truly felt like it was the first time he had fallen in love.

As they walked back from the restaurant he lagged behind on purpose. He had to tell her about dinner. She loved hearing pointless random details about what went on in his life. He sat on a bench and messaged.

"Dinner was good but very cheesy n greasy. So stuffed."

Within a few seconds, he had her response.

"I will dump you if you get fat."

She followed it with a winking emoji. She loved those emojis. He sent her some crazy ones in return.

He imagined her laughing at their nonsensical banter. He imagined her smile, it lit up everything inside him. He was so lost in the back n forth that he didn't notice Sid standing in front of him. He imagined holding her sweet face in his hands and tears welled up in his eyes. He couldn't see the phone screen anymore.

As he turned his face up to clear his eyes, he saw Sid looking at his hands. At the two phones that he held. It was too late to hide them. He let them fall to the ground, along with his tears.

"It's almost been a year since she died. Let go!"

GREED

The tube light flickered intermittently and Sharad fluttered his eyes, trying to match every flicker. He drummed his fingers on the desk and then fidgeted with the edge of the collar of his worn-out white cotton shirt, running his fingers down the blue stripes. And lastly, he ran his hands along his thighs, tracing the crease of his faded black trousers. He had run out of mindless things to do.

It was not like he was free or bored. On the contrary, he had way too much work. He was frustrated. Sharad could never say no to anyone and people took advantage of that. People took advantage of a lot of things, things that Sharad stayed away from, like opportunities to make an extra buck. His boss Mr Gill and his colleague Chirag were pros at it. They had tried to include him in their team on a tricky project a year ago, one that promised a truckload of dirty money. But since his refusal to participate in their misdeeds, they had not only excluded him from their shenanigans but tried their best to make his life as miserable as they possibly could.

That was the price Sharad had to pay for sticking to his values. Mr Gill always saddled him with all the undesirable projects and doubled his responsibilities. Being pretty low on the corporate ladder, there wasn't much that Sharad could do to counter or avoid it. Not that he would have done anything even if he could. He just wanted to stay out of trouble.

Chirag passed Sharad's desk as he headed toward Mr Gill's room. With a smirk on his face he commented. "You look busy today."

Sharad looked up at Chirag and all he could see was a stylish blazer, shiny shoes, and a fancy watch. The man himself seemed shadowed by his possessions, not something Sharad ever desired for himself. He shook his head, let the snide remark pass and got back to what he did best, his job.

***

Propped up with a bunch of pillows and the new bestseller from his favourite author in his hands, Sharad was on the verge of falling asleep when Divya came running and jumped right on top of his belly. She was full of energy, as any six year old would be. But she was a lot more mature for her age than one would expect.

"Can I have a doll house Puppa, the big one?" She stretched her tiny hands as wide apart as she could. She had a cheeky smile on her face and her eyes twinkled but she was careful to ensure that her tone was polite.

Sharad gave her a tight hug. "Yes my baby, it can be your Diwali gift."

"As if we have loads to spend on Diwali. My *pooja* list itself is incomplete, how are you even talking about gifts!" Neha had followed Divya into the room. She flung the kitchen rag on the chair and crawled into bed with them. Her long wavy hair was tied in a loose low knot. Unknowingly she brushed her bindi to one side as she wiped the sweat off her forehead with her sari.

"We should not have started work on your parents' house. It's eating up all the money." She lay her head on Sharad's shoulder as she said this. She avoided meeting his eyes whenever she spoke on this topic.

Sharad sighed. "You know we had to do this, my parents couldn't keep living in that broken down place. It needed to be fixed."

"I know, but what about us? You know you can make some extra money but you just refuse to do it. You and your stupid morals!" She lifted her head and moved away, crossing her arms in defiance.

She didn't look very different from Divya, sulking in anger.

Sharad couldn't help but smile at her childish behaviour. He had heard enough from her over the last year about money and how he should have agreed to work with his boss. But he knew it mainly came from her frustration at money being tight all the time, she didn't truly mean it. But it was slowly eating away at him, that she wasn't entirely wrong, money was an issue.

"So what colour doll house do you want Divya?" He tickled his little angel as she giggled and jumped all over him. And soon Neha joined in as all three rolled on the bed together.

****

The opulence of the room was in stark contrast to the rest of the office. Garish decorations lined the shelves, an antique clock proudly adorned the blue wall and a long ignored mini-golf set lay gathering dust in one corner.

"I trust you more than anyone else Sharad, that's why I am asking you to do this." Mr Gill was at his solemn and sincere best. Sharad wasn't buying his nonsense but he listened quietly, and in any case, he didn't have much of an option. Instead, he focused on admiring Mr Gill's acting abilities.

The ignorant man continued, still quite seriously. "The money had to be wired but something went wrong. You will need to hand it over yourself to our contact in Mumbai, Mr Shah."

"How much is it?" Sharad cut straight to the chase. He knew it was all a pack of lies, scripted with Chirag possibly.

His boss tossed over a small brown packet. "An amount you will never see or earn in your whole life. Be extra careful. Don't mess it up for me or you will be in deep shit." The nice guy act was over now.

As Sharad weighed the packet in his hand he thought to himself. "It's another one of your sordid money deals. You can't trust anyone else with the money can you, especially not Chirag."

His boss had very cleverly planned the whole deal under the guise of an official errand and Sharad had no way of squeezing out of this one, no matter how reluctant he was to be a part of it. He had to figure out ways to avoid getting trapped in such situations but till then he had to do his bidding.

He felt like punching Mr Gill's smug face but that was something he just wasn't capable of. He had half a mind to throw the packet in the bin but all he could manage was a timid glare as he exited the room with the tainted money in his hands.

****

"Yes, *Baba*. I will arrange for something. It might take some time though. It's not a small amount." Sharad had the speaker phone on while packing his suitcase. His train was late in the evening, an overnight journey. But he wanted to be done with his packing soon so that he could spend some time with Divya.

Neha folded a shirt and quietly handed it over to Sharad as he disconnected the call, he could sense the tension in the air. He normally avoided money discussions in front of her and knew a comment was headed his way.

"So the contractor wants more money now? It's never-ending. Money is just pouring into the repairs like crazy. What will you do?"

Sharad quietly went about keeping his things. He refused to respond to Neha although frustration was boiling up inside him. "I will keep my shaving kit and brush in the bag instead of the suitcase, it will be easier to take out in the morning."

They both pretended to focus on the packing for some time before Neha threw his shirt on the bed and let herself go. "What about us Sharad? When will we have money for us? Why do you have to be the only good guy around? When will you think of us?"

Sharad finally lost it too and shouted at her. "I will figure it out. Leave me alone, just get out of here."

With tears stinging her eyes Neha rushed out of the room. Cursing his behaviour Sharad held the packet of money in his hands and stared at it for a long time. He could hear his father's desperate voice, coupled with the vision of Neha in tears. As he heard Divya call out to him, he quickly shut the suitcase. He would put the money in the suitcase carefully later, he told himself. Throwing the brown paper packet under his pillow, Sharad went after his bundle of joy.

****

Divya chased him around the sofa tirelessly but Sharad needed to sit for a moment and take some time out. Spending time with Divya always cheered him up and kept all thoughts of trouble at bay. But today he just couldn't get things out of his mind. Neha's words haunted him, and he felt she wasn't entirely wrong. He finally sat down on the sofa and Divya crept up next to him, perched on the cushions, she held his arm tight. They sat in silence till Neha placed a cup of tea in front of him. "I have packed your dinner, you can eat on the train."

Sharad stroked Divya's hair as she hung on to his arm, pulling at his fingers playfully. He didn't want to say anything to Neha in front of her. But he wanted to sort things out with her before he left.

"Baby can you go and put Puppa's food in his bag? Then go and wash your hands and face for dinner." Neha said as she gently pried Divya off her father. She wanted to talk alone with Sharad too.

As Divya ran off into the bedroom with Sharad's dinner, Neha sat beside him. She took his hands in hers and smiled lovingly. "I am sorry. I didn't mean any of it. I don't want you to get all tense. Let's leave all this. You just do your work."

Sharad squeezed her hands and smiled back. She had a good heart, she deserved better in life. That's when it happened, clarity hit him hard like a bolt out of the blue. He decided he would keep the money. He didn't know how he would explain it to Mr Gill but he knew he had to do this. And that's all he thought about as he went about preparing to leave.

Divya ran into his arms as he put his luggage in the taxi. "Can we buy the doll house when you are back, I don't want to wait for Diwali?"

"Yes my sweety, we most definitely will." Said Sharad confidently as he thought of the money lying under his pillow. He hadn't said a word to Neha yet. He knew that she wouldn't let him do this no matter what she said in her misery. He would have to do this by himself. His heart already felt lighter as the taxi pulled away and he waved back at the smiling faces of his wife and daughter.

***

The train had started pulling away slowly from the station, Sharad had to push through the thronging friends and family that crowded the platform. The whistle pierced his ears as he grabbed hold of the bar at the door of a carriage and jumped into it. Despite having started from home well in time, the crawling traffic had delayed him. As he went from carriage to carriage looking for his seat, he wondered if it was a sign, that he should not have boarded the train without the money. That he should not have pandered to his wild thoughts. But then he decided to focus on the fact that he had made it to the train despite the obstacles, that was the sign he preferred. He was meant to do this.

As he settled into his berth next to the window he was lost in his thoughts again, on how to handle the fact that he would have no money to show to Mr Gill's contact. He couldn't just say that he had lost it. They could literally kill him if he didn't have a solid story to back him up. He knew he wouldn't be getting any sleep that night.

His musings were interrupted by an incoherent mumbling and Sharad felt someone poking at his outstretched legs. It was a beggar in filthy rags. His hair was long and matted like a *sadhu* but more from unhygienic conditions than anything spiritual. He wasn't old but had a bent back, smelt like rotten food and half his teeth were missing. Sharad's first instinct was to push him off with his feet.

The beggar backed off a bit and said in an unexpectedly hurt and defiant tone. "You don't have to push, just give me some money and I will be on my way."

Sharad pulled his bag and suitcase closer to him and sternly told him to move on. At that, the beggar sneered at him and eyed his luggage. Taking a few steps to move ahead, he stopped dramatically for a few seconds and turned his head back, flinging his unwashed tresses around his shoulders. With his nose up in the air he snarled at Sharad. "Being greedy won't get you anywhere!"

Although he was taken aback by the insolence and surprisingly haughty demeanour of the beggar, an idea started to form in Sharad's mind. He ran after the beggar and caught up with him at the door of the carriage. He held himself back as he saw the man hanging on lightly to the bars, dangerously close to the world that sped by outside. He didn't seem very bothered about falling off. He probably didn't have much worth caring about in life. But Sharad did.

He approached the open door cautiously and stood next to the beggar. They spent the next twenty minutes in deep conversation. Sharad did all the talking, explaining what he wanted the beggar to do the next morning, going into minute details as the beggar listened to him earnestly. When he was certain the beggar had understood, he took out a thousand rupees and put them in the his hands, and closed the deal. The beggar's eyes lit up. He smiled at Sharad, the darkness of his mouth lighting up the handful of teeth left in there. Things seemed to have turned for him and he moved a bit away from the door as if life was precious again.

Sharad went back and took out his dinner from the bag. He smiled as he eyed his suitcase and thought of his plan. It might just work. He couldn't wait to reach Mumbai the next morning.

****

As the train pulled into the station Sharad was wide awake and ready with his luggage. He made sure a few other passengers got off before him so that there were enough people on the platform. As he stepped off the train, he deliberately placed his suitcase right next to a family standing near him. A middle-aged man was discussing breakfast options with his wife while their teenage son looked around for more exciting things in life. A porter was eyeing him, hoping Sharad would ask for his assistance. That was a good thing, he was being watched.

Sharad started fumbling as if looking for something in his pocket. His eyes darted around, looking for the beggar. Unable to spot him, he wondered if the beggar might have run off with his thousand rupees. He felt stupid at having overlooked this detail, how could he have trusted him. He hoped a suitcase would provide additional incentive to the beggar to fulfil the deal.

Panic started setting in now. The train would move soon and all the people would disperse, the platform would soon be empty He didn't have much time. But just as hope was slipping away, he heard the teenager shout. "Hey stop!"

Sharad turned just in time to see the beggar making off with his suitcase. He screamed as loud as he could. "Stop, that's my suitcase."

He started to chase after him as all the people around looked at the two of them running. The beggar was doing a great job, hugging the suitcase tight, matted tresses flying in the air, he even bumped into a couple of people as he made for his escape. Sharad hoped those people would still be around in case the police wanted to talk to witnesses. Soon he slowed down and let the beggar slip away. He even tripped on nothing and fell as hard as he could to lend more authenticity to the situation. Sharad was thankful there were not too many people around, but those who were had gotten a good look at the whole incident. And for once he was glad nobody had the conscience or courage to help him out. The beggar had made a clean getaway.

"You should go to the Railway Police." Belated morality had kicked into the porter and he had somehow managed to catch up with Sharad. He even helped him up to his feet, brushing the dust off him.

Sharad tried to look as helpless as he could. "Could you help me, please? I am new here. I had some very important things in that suitcase."

The porter led him to the Railway Police office. Sharad stepped in and prepared to lie his heart out.

****

Things went much smoother with the police than Sharad had thought. He had been expecting a long wait, a barrage of questions, and possibly even a request for some cash to move things forward. But none of that transpired, it was possibly something you only saw in a movie. They were least interested in him or in finding his suitcase. Much to Sharad's relief, this case was surely not worth their time and they readily dismissed him after filing a report.

Now came the tricky part. He still had to connect with Mr Gill's contact person. Putting an official copy of the FIR in his bag he decided to see his plan through. It was not like he could return without meeting this man. Sharad walked all the way to Mr Shah's office, using this time to think his story through and make sure he made no mistakes. He entered the dilapidated building and took the stairs to the third floor. The office itself was neat and clean although extremely sparse. A young man who looked like he had stepped right out of a gangster movie, led him to his boss. His gold chains and tattoos glared at Sharad and the angular bulge in his pant pocket seemed to be aiming right at him.

Mr Shah himself looked harmless with a lanky, frail body hiding behind a simple white *kurta* and brown pants. His short hair was lightly oiled and patted neatly over his head. His eyes were soft but alert and even his thin moustache was not menacing. It was his calm that disturbed Sharad.

Sha' Bhai, as the young henchman had called him, looked intently at the FIR when Sharad told him the whole story and handed over proof that he had been robbed. The boss did not react in any way, his demeanour remained serene. He got up from his chair and walked to the front of the table, uncomfortably close to Sharad. Resting his back on the table, he deliberately let the report slip down to the ground, floating slowly towards Sharad's feet. Where it belonged. He took out his phone and dialled Mr Gill's number.

"Your man is screwing with us. He says he has been robbed. Apparently, there were witnesses and he also has some police report." He took a long pause for no reason whatsoever and then continued in his monotonous voice laced with a slight hint of threat. "I don't care if it's true or not. I want my money."

Without another word, he handed the phone to Sharad. Before he could say anything Mr Gill screamed from the other end. "What are you trying to do to me Sharad? Where is the damn money?"

Sharad almost had a grin on his face. He knew his boss could not do a thing. He had all his alibis and proof in place. And besides, there was no way Mr Gill could go to the police himself, that money was totally black.

"I am sorry Sir but you can check with the police and witnesses. It might even be in the local papers tomorrow."

Sharad was almost as calm as Sha' Bhai who had now totally lost interest in him, just like the police, and walked out of the room. Mr Gill wasn't listening to a word of what Sharad had to say, he was on a trip of his own. "You are fired. Don't bother coming back. If I see you again I will ruin you. You cannot work in this town ever again."

Sharad wondered. "Do I need to work anymore?" And he cut the call.

****

The cool breeze blew in Sharad's face and he sat on the edge of the seat trying to get as much air as he could. It snapped him out of the myriad thoughts swirling in his head. As the autorickshaw hurtled down the road, he was constantly pinching himself. Luckily for Sharad, he was small fry in Sha' Bhai's eyes, Mr Gill being his main focus. He couldn't believe how easily he had just walked out of the gangster's lair, alive. His plan had worked. He held his breath for a long time, almost too scared to heave a sigh of relief. As he headed back to the station to take the next train home he thought of any loopholes he might have missed, anything he may have overlooked.

As he took out his wallet to pay the rickshaw driver it struck him, he realised that he had left the packet with the money lying around at home without having told Neha. He kicked at a stone in frustration at this mistake but quickly gathered his wits. He had to call Neha right away and tell her to put it away safely. He didn't have an option but to get her involved now.

"Yes, I reached safely Neha, listen to me please first." Sharad was finding it hard to get even a word in. Neha was happy to hear from him and wanted to enquire about his well-being, she was used to being the one who did all the talking.

"Were the *puris* OK? I think I put too much salt in the *bhaaji*."

"Neha!" Sharad tried his best to keep from screaming.

"Were you able to sleep at all, I know you find trains quite uncomfortable?"

"Nehaaaa!" Sharad was close to crushing the phone in his hand now.

"Was the place easy... to...?" Sensing an increasing gravity in Sharad's tone, Neha finally cut herself short.

"Now listen to me carefully. Remember that packet I got from the office. It is lying under my pillow. Go and put it safely inside the cupboard right away." He instructed her carefully and slowly, stressing on each word.

Neha exclaimed and her questions burst forth once again. "What? You forgot to take the packet! Are you sure?"

Sharad could now hear some rustling sounds. "Yes, I have checked my bag properly. Find it and put it away?"

"It's not there. I am looking for it. Are you certain you left it under the pillow?" Neha sounded confused.

Sharad could feel the sweat forming on his brow, his breathing got heavier. Staying calm was getting harder and harder.

"Look properly!" His voice was agitated now and passers-by were staring at him. He asked her random questions. Did anyone else come into the room, had the maid come yet, had she changed the sheets. He was panicking now.

"Nobody has come Sharad. You only left last night and it's still morning. Relax. I will look for it and call you back." Neha cut the phone without waiting for a response from him, totally unaware of the turmoil he was going through.

All kinds of thoughts went through Sharad's mind and he couldn't focus. He kept staring at his phone waiting for Neha to call. He decided to start walking to the ticket counter, as if buying a train ticket would get him home faster. But he had to do something, just waiting for Neha to revert was only increasing his anxiety.

As he reached the ticket counter the phone rang. Sharad turned away immediately and went to a corner. Without waiting to hear a hello, he almost shouted. "Did you find it?"

Neha's composed response relaxed him. "Don't worry, it's safe."

Sharad shut his eyes and let out a sigh. He even smiled at the man at the ticket counter who looked at him in a rather amused manner. His heartbeat was slowly coming back to normal. He managed to stroll leisurely as he chatted with Neha.

"So, where did you find it?"

"Actually, Divya found it. She's such a clever girl." Neha's voice was full of pride.

Sharad also couldn't help but smile. They both doted on their daughter. They laughed as they joked that Divya deserved a treat for saving the day.

Sharad shook his head in disbelief and relief as he headed to a bench near the entrance. He had not caught a moment's rest since this whole charade had begun. He could feel the weariness slowly creeping into his body. He thought of his parent's house, Neha's Diwali list, and most importantly Divya's doll house. He closed his eyes and managed a wry smile. But it wasn't over yet. The money wouldn't be safe at home but he would figure that out once he was back. And then there was Mr Gill to manage. Till then Neha had to take care of things.

"Where did you keep it? It needs to be extremely safe. It's a very big amount."

But Neha wasn't listening to him at all, she was lost in praising her clever little girl.

"Oh, it's perfectly safe. When Divya put the food in your bag last evening, she saw the packet under the pillow. She had figured out that it was important for you. And very smartly she put it inside your suitcase. It's right there, with you!"

The phone dropped from Sharad's hands as Neha's voice trailed off. His legs buckled under him and he fell to the floor, the beggar's words ringing in his ears!

Destiny

Randy's eyes opened wide as his heart pounded faster and faster. His breathing became heavier, as his muscular chest heaved up and down rapidly. He clenched his fists tight as he spotted her hiding in the bathroom. Shivering and crouching, trying to block the door with her fragile body. But he noticed something she didn't. The skinny arm of a young child dangling from the bathtub behind her, a delicate charms bracelet tied around the wrist. A flower, a pony, a few stars, and a tiny little ice cream cone, blood dripping from it onto the floor.

Tears were streaming down the woman's beautiful face, her short black hair ran amok around her head. But it was the terror in her eyes that made him want to reach out to her. To hold her in his arms and save her from the horrific night that saw no end. But he couldn't. And even though it pained him and scared him, he wanted to find out how she would take it. He wanted to see her reaction, her pain.

It was that strange sadistic pleasure that humans get at times from watching others in misery that kept him going. Nobody ever admits it but every one of us has gone through it. And Randy wanted more, he did not want it to stop. The bathroom door was flung open with a brutal kick. The terrified young woman was thrown to the floor. As she slithered and retreated towards the bathtub, pleading incoherently for her life, she touched the dangling arm. Despite the madman in front of her, she involuntarily turned around. Her eyes took in the bracelet with the bloodied charms and she let out a heart-rending shriek.

Randy almost screamed himself and fell off the edge of the couch. But his reaction was not to the woman screaming on the TV screen, but to the sound of a window suddenly slamming shut in the kitchen. He was pretty sure he had closed all doors and windows when it started drizzling, just as he had put on the movie. His Friday night horror indulgence, a weekly ritual. The ratings and reviews were irrelevant, just watching people getting butchered was all he needed to get that high.

And right now he was not happy at having to stop the movie just as the woman was about to meet a gruesome end. But he had to prevent the water from flooding his kitchen. As he walked in, he noticed a thick furry tail slink out of the window.

Fury written all over his face, Randy pulled the window shut in frustration and bolted it up tight.

"That bloody cat, it's always snooping around." His anger was rising now and he needed a smoke to calm himself down. Grabbing his hoodie and pocketing his house keys, Randy stepped out into the light shower. He wasn't very fond of the damp smell of wet clothes but he did enjoy the soft pelting of raindrops on his face. As he lit the cigarette his nose twitched at a stench that wafted towards him with the wind. He grimaced and peered hard into the night to see where it was coming from. It didn't take him long to figure it out, at the base of the sole bush in his small unkempt garden lay the mangled remains of an unidentifiable small animal. This wasn't the first time.

Randy was pretty certain who the culprit was, that fat brown cat with two silver streaks across her eyes, always roaming around his property. She somehow seemed to grace only his house with her unwelcome visits. If only he could get his hands on her, or better still, the cat's owner, the bloody alcoholic. Randy kicked a final bit of dirt over the rotting carcass and looked up to the apartments opposite his house. The lights were on in the house where that feline lived. Although he couldn't see anyone he felt like he was being watched. In a show of defiance, he pushed back his hood roughly and scowled at the window blinds, brows knotted in murderous anger. Then he quickly turned around and stomped back into his house to finish the movie. He would have to make do with only the pretty woman dying tonight.

***

The gnarled branch of a tree tapped a code on the window in vain. One could see the whole neighbourhood through it. The cars coming and going, people walking by, lives going on incessantly all around. The window was in a corner of the bedroom on the first-floor apartment. It was situated such that although one could clearly see everything on the streets, it was not that noticeable the other way around. The outside world couldn't access the life inside this room that easily. It was the perfect setting to indulge in some voyeurism without getting noticed.

The laptop perched on the edge of the table at this window hummed softly, the mechanical sound that comes out of machines, sometimes jarring, sometimes soothing.

"He was wearing his favourite pair of jeans with an oversized black shirt that kept his well-toned body hidden. It was good to be on holiday. The sun, the sand, and the sea, no matter how cliché, it worked for him!"

Only these lines had been typed in the last twenty minutes. Anuj sat gazing at the smudge on the wall, his eyes squinting in concentration, occasionally blowing at the long limp hair that fell into his eyes. Although it wasn't too warm thanks to the rain from the previous night, the sweat had caused his t-shirt to turn a darker shade of grey around the neck.

He was lost in memories of his beach holiday with Jay. A holiday he had hoped would break the writer's block that he seemed to have had for the last four years. But it had been three days since they had returned and he had not even gone beyond one page. He wondered if he lied to himself when he said that writing was his life.

"You're the luckiest, who gets to do what they always dreamed of as a career!" His mother would always make it a point to say that when he went home for a visit. "He was born to be a writer!" She would proudly tell anyone who cared to listen, and even those who did not. As if writing the weekly column in a local newspaper was the same as winning the Pulitzer. He wondered who was in greater denial, him or his mother.

"Writer indeed!" Anuj exclaimed in a loud voice, making Paws jump out of her slumber. She purred but did not move an inch, the laziest cat he had ever seen but just the right low maintenance companion he needed. Jay always joked about how unimaginatively he had named her, being a writer and all.

"Don't I look handsome with that smirk on my face?" He asked her, baring all his teeth and raising an eyebrow. "Girls like that bad boy look you know!" He poked her fat belly and ran his fingers across the silver streaks on her eyes. Paws couldn't be bothered to even purr, thoroughly enjoying the pampering.

"You need to stop your clandestine romantic meetings with Randy you know, the way he glares at me. He might just kill us both someday!"

Anuj laughed at his lame joke and brought his attention back to the writing. Pushing Paws' tail off the keyboard he started thumping at the keys again. He had to get out of this self pity mode and do what he was 'born to do'. A hot cup of coffee would possibly help.

As he filled up the kettle he spotted the brandy bottle. With a longing glance, he shut the cabinet door on it and went back to his laptop. A conversation with Paws may take his mind off his melancholy.

"Do girls ever fall for good guys like me?" Paws seemed to move her head in answer and it certainly was not a nod.

***

Anuj was absolutely at ease with the work-from-home scenario, all alone. Jay had offered to move in with him after the binge incident but he had refused. He believed that he wrote better when by himself. He would sit every evening at his laptop and try to write those amazing stories he knew existed somewhere in his head.

Anuj's stomach rumbled and he realised that he didn't have anything to eat for dinner. And he wasn't in the mood to cook, as was mostly the case. He slipped into his sandals and grabbed his wallet as he rushed out to the supermarket across the road. Some pita bread and humus would do for today. He remembered just in time that he was out of wine. He had relegated his drinking to only wines in the last few months as they seemed to agree with his system much better. Apart from the fact that Jay had insisted that he take a break from hard liquor after he had lost control that one day. And it was a Saturday, he felt like creating at least the semblance of a party if nothing else.

Lost in thought he ambled down the liquor aisle and bumped right into a girl coming from the other end. She dropped some packets of chips as she fumbled to save the wine bottle in her hand. Anuj quickly fell to the floor to pick her things up. As they both kneeled down, Anuj stared at her shamelessly, unaware of his behaviour. She had shoulder length black hair with red streaks. Eyes lined with a thick liner. Dark red lipstick. Her dress matched her lips and hair. A slim short black skirt and a sleeveless sparkly red top. She looked all set to paint the town an obvious red.

She decided to ignore his brash stare. "Thank you." She said. "By the way, the Zinfandel is a pretty good wine, if you would like to try." Her voice was soft yet bold. She waited a minute for Anuj to respond, but he was tongue tied as usual. To break the awkwardness she pointed with her dainty fingers to the wine bottle she held. "This one!"

He noticed the silver bracelet on her wrist, the bells on it jangled and shook him out of his trance, and he mumbled. "Thanks, I will try it out." And they parted ways casting shy glances at each other.

As Anuj stepped out of the store with his things, he couldn't help but look around for the girl he had bumped into. He wished he had spoken to her, asked her name, maybe even got her number. But he knew that was exceedingly ambitious thinking on his part.

It was getting pretty dark outside now but was lit enough for him to spot her standing next to a flashy silver grey sedan. She was busy peering into her phone. Anuj wondered if he had just been presented with an opportunity to follow through on his musings. But before he could take a step in her direction he saw a tall, thin man walk towards her. He had a brown leather jacket on with a peace symbol on the back. It was hard to see his face from a distance but he looked older than the girl, possibly middle-aged. As the man slipped into the driver's seat the girl looked up for a brief moment. Their eyes met, she raised her hand in acknowledgement and smiled. As the sedan zoomed away, Anuj decided to make do with the lovely smile that had just come his way, even that was a blue moon in his life.

****

Anuj woke up with a start to the sound of a clattering pan on the floor. Paws must have knocked something over in the kitchen, the cat seriously needed to hit the gym he thought. As he tried to get out of bed his head spun like a top. He must have had a few more glasses than intended the previous night. With a lot of effort he managed to get to the bathroom and splash some water on his face.

Just meeting that girl had given Anuj a high. He felt happy. He felt inspired. He had poured himself a glass of the Zinfandel which certainly was as delicious as the girl had promised it would be. And then he had rushed to his laptop, raring to write his masterpiece. What better than a story woven around the girl. Yes, that's what he would write about, a love story with a mysterious beautiful girl in it. Anuj remembered punching away, his imagination in overdrive, and his glass always full.

Beyond that, he could not recall a thing and now it was eleven in the morning, he never slept this late. His face tingled from the cold splash. He poured himself a hot coffee and settled down on the couch with Paws curled around his leg.

He rifled idly through the papers, as always, skipping his own column. His turtle mind took some time to register the headlines, he was already on page three by then. And when it did, he rushed back to the front page and read the headline properly. It made him wince: 'Gruesome Murder of Young Girl in City'.

As he read the description of the victim, his heart sank.

'The victim was a young girl in her early twenties. She had shoulder length black hair with red streaks. Traces of dark red lipstick on her lips, she was dressed in a short black skirt and a sleeveless red top. A silver bracelet lay by her side.'

Anuj's hands shook as he forced himself to read all the details.

'She was found lying next to the highway in a pool of blood. Her throat had been slit and her clothes

were ripped. It appears, she put up a fight before the assailant cut her throat, as she had many bruises over her arms and legs.'

Anuj flung the newspaper down as hard as he could. He couldn't believe that it could be the same girl. It had to be a coincidence. He paced around the house for a while, fussed over Paws, and did all he could to get his mind off this terrible incident. When nothing worked he decided to get back to the story, maybe the theme of love in his work would help calm his mind.

As he opened the document and read the last paragraph he had written, a chill went down his spine.

"She fought the man with all her might. Although he was not strongly built, the tall, thin man overpowered her easily. Her clothes tore as she tried to grapple with him. There wasn't much room in the car for movement. She soon tired out. Her mascara ran down her cheeks with her tears. Just as she let up her fight for a moment, he got his chance. The man grabbed his knife and slit her throat in one shot. Before she could even scream, he reached over, opened her door, and pushed her onto the side of the highway. The silver grey sedan vanished into the misty road ahead."

Anuj rushed to the bathroom to throw up.

✳✳✳

It was hours before Anuj could muster up the courage to face the screen once again. His mind was a mangle of thoughts and questions. He couldn't believe it, he was certain that was not what he had written the night before. He was writing about love and romance, not murder. How did it change. Was it the wine, did he get drunk, did he change the storyline later. But most importantly, had it somehow come true!

Anuj had always enjoyed the freedom of his solitude, going by his moods, moving chores around, and fitting things around his schedule. Being a loner, he didn't even miss the company of humans. But today, the last thing he wanted was to be alone. So when the doorbell rang, he wasted no time getting to the door. He was thankful that Jay had decided to drop by for a while.

Jay had always been there for him when he was bullied in school, when he was made fun of in college, and when he had lost himself in alcohol in recent times. It was Jay who helped him come out of that drunk weekend when he had gone over the top and nearly stepped in front of a bus. Jay had handled his mother, his workplace, and of course, Anuj himself. There was much to thank him for!

The previous night's happenings had quite the opposite effect on Jay though. He seemed quite amused by it all and was pretty certain it was just a coincidence. "It's that silly writer in you that's getting all dramatic. You need to chill a bit."

Jay's confidence rubbed off on him and he started feeling calmer. Jay had that effect on people, friends, girls, strangers, just about anyone. Anuj admired and envied, in equal measure, Jay's many charismatic traits.

With an important meeting lined up the next morning, Jay took his leave in order to sleep early but not before giving Anuj an interesting idea. Quite possibly, more to placate him than from any real exploration. He suggested that Anuj write again tonight and see what happens, whether it comes true the next day or not. That might help settle the matter. The idea appealed to Anuj and he headed back to his laptop as dusk fell.

After deleting the document from the previous night, he started a new one, He had two clear objectives in mind, the writing had to be fictional and non-violent. He typed and deleted with equal fervour, never going beyond a few lines. His brain refused to cooperate somehow. He gazed outside his window at the empty street, surfed the net, and rifled through books, but nothing worked.

He was so engrossed in kick-starting his brain that he took ages to realise Paws was pawing at him in frustration. It was way beyond her dinner time. While opening the tuna can for her, his eyes travelled back to the half-empty bottle of brandy at the edge of the cabinet.

Paws settled down on the window sill after her hearty dinner and Anuj was at the table with a brandy by his side. It worked, the words were flowing now. He wrote about a young man, fresh out of college. His life in the city, his adventures, and how he embarks on a new journey. This was way more than he had written in months and Anuj felt elated. The writing reflected his mood, full of life and energy. As the brandy decreased, the words increased. And Anuj wrote the night away.

****

For a change, it was not a sudden noise nor the alarm that woke Anuj up. The warmth of the sunlight streaming through the window engulfed him in a hug. He felt rested and peaceful. Paws reflected his calm state, staring lazily into his eyes while she lay next to him on the pillow. Anuj was tempted to enjoy relaxing in bed for some more time but the sight of his laptop shook him out of his slumber. Pushing Paws aside, he rushed to get the papers.

He wasn't sure what he was looking for but he wanted to go through them anyway. He stood right at the door and rummaged through, too impatient to even get back inside. There was nothing, except one line, that the police were investigating the murder of the girl found on Saturday night and had made no headway. He had a fleeting feeling of guilty disappointment. But then he laughed at himself for making such a big deal of this coincidence.

As he was about to shut his door he noticed sounds in the apartment to his right. It had been empty for nearly two months and Anuj certainly did not miss the noisy occupants that were kicked out unceremoniously by the landlord based on an 'anonymous' complaint.

Stretching his neck to look further, he nearly got hit by a big cardboard box being carried by a man headed towards the neighbouring apartment. "Hi, are you moving in?" He asked the burly man. Not one for words, the man just pointed behind him with his thumb and rushed into the house to offload the heavy box.

Anuj looked back and saw a young man approaching. The man seemed in his late thirties, maybe just a few years older than himself. He was of stocky build, rather handsome, wearing jeans and a tight solid-blue shirt. His dark maroon leather shoes had low heels which clicked as he walked across the hall. His hair was cropped short and had two stylish zig-zag lines razored in on either side.

He gave Anuj a friendly smile as he almost passed by, suddenly stopping in his tracks, as if on second thoughts. He looked straight into Anuj's eyes and pointed his fingers at him with two loaded thumbs. "Neighbour?"

Anuj was a bit amused at the man's chilled out cowboy attitude. In fact, he kind of liked him, anyone who was not like Randy was welcome anyway. Before he could react, the 'cowboy' gave him a quick salute with his left hand and walked off. This light encounter cheered Anuj up and he left the papers at the door. He was certain he had not had too much to drink and that was the reason he was feeling a whole lot better. He made a mental note to drink less, it really did not suit him. It was possibly firing up his imagination the wrong way. And back to work it was for him, this fine Monday morning.

But all the peace and calm vanished the moment he sat at his desk. His laptop stared back at him fiercely. With words that had surely not emanated from his brain. The fun young lead character from last night was gone and so were his adventures.

Anuj shivered as he read the lines that had appeared in place of the original writing.

"After the attack, the killer had to lay low for a while. A change of location would possibly help, the

other side of town preferably. He would have to try to blend in with the neighbours, and make new friends. He would even have to change his appearance."

Anuj swallowed hard, suddenly feeling scared. Very scared. The document went on to describe the killer's new looks. The detailing was unmistakable, down to the hairstyle and boots, he knew this cowboy already. Anuj glanced towards the shared wall as if to look through into the house next door. Despite the fear, he started growing more curious about the whole experience now. And somehow, he even started enjoying it in a creepy way. Or was it his way of dealing with the nightmare he seemed to be living in right now.

Anuj thought hard and came up with a strategy. He would not move out of the house until he was sure about his new neighbour, keeping a watch on him at all times. And secondly, he decided to do something about his writing and the chain of events that somehow he seemed to have triggered. He would do it differently this time. He knew he couldn't write even a few lines without drinking. So he decided to get drunk first this time and then write without knowing what he wanted to write. It seemed to change anyway so it shouldn't matter, he convinced himself.

Paws watched intently as Anuj went about preparing for battle. He set a bottle of vodka next to the laptop, the one he had hidden away for a rainy day. He put on a pair of socks to keep warm and put his phone on silent. Instead of his usual slow sips, he gulped down three shots, one after the other. His throat burned but he felt empowered and confident. And his fingers started twitching.

****

Anuj woke up with a heavy head, but he seemed to be getting used to this state. He managed to get out of bed without stumbling. He didn't remember a word of what he wrote last night. Without bothering to even wash his face he ran to his laptop. Not knowing what to expect, he sat in anticipation as the screen flickered alive. And his eyes fell on the one and only line on the whole page.

"The cat deserves to die!"

"Paws!" Anuj screamed at the top of his voice unable to move even an inch from his chair. Almost paralysed with fear and concern, he somehow pulled himself up and ran to all the rooms, looked behind every curtain and under every piece of furniture. As he made his way back to the laptop he noticed that the window was open. Anuj never left this window open as Paws would crawl out onto the tree and settle down there. It was nearly impossible to get her back inside once that happened. He felt a flicker of relief at the thought of seeing her languishing on one of the branches. But the branches lay empty, even the leaves had fallen off and left the tree bare.

Crestfallen, Anuj swept his gaze across the neighbourhood in vain. He did not dare step out of the house. This was all wrong, very wrong. Sitting in a corner of the room he spent nearly the whole day waiting to hear a meow.

As darkness took over, Anuj shook himself out of his misery and went back to shut the window. A draught was seeping in and it had started getting chilly. In any case, Paws usually came and went through the pet door and not the window. He had not given up hope yet, he knew she would come back sooner or later. She always did.

He had almost started feeling hopeful again but his mood did an about turn as he spotted Randy from the window. And he wasn't alone, the new neighbour was standing with him. They seemed lost in conversation when Randy suddenly looked up in his direction and gave his usual smirk. This made the cowboy turn around too and flash his charming smile. Only this time, the smile seemed laced with a hint of evil and a dash of Randy's smirk. The last straw was when he turned back, and Anuj spotted the peace symbol on the brown leather jacket.

Something flipped in Anuj's mind. He lost all his cool but also, partly his fear. He had to do something about this. He couldn't just sit and wait for things to go wrong again. He decided he would write with the purpose of getting the murderer caught, whoever it was. A new plot started hatching in his mind. Unable to contain his nervous excitement, he called up Jay to discuss things with him.

To his surprise, Anuj felt that Jay was taking him seriously this time and that reassured him to a certain extent.

"Let's plan this out in detail, the deeper you have it thought out in your mind, the better it will translate into the written word."

Anuj couldn't agree more. "We should get it straight, even the dialogues, the clothes, everything."

Between the two of them, they planned it down to the last detail. Anuj would write about how the police catch the culprit and lock him up. He would think it through properly before typing it out this time, no more unplanned writing and no going with the flow. He would stick to a pre-thought story. Jay also rightly advised him to control the drinking, and to have only as much as was needed to get the writing going.

Anuj would have to be mentally strong, he had to take his chance on this and do something about that dangerous man. So he poured himself a drink and sat to write after he had the whole plot chalked out in his mind.

"The Inspector was sharp and had finally put two and two together, they had got their man. The very next morning the murderer was in handcuffs and thrown into prison for the crimes he had committed."

The story had shaped up well, and Anuj was pleased with himself. He even felt proud at spinning something of a pot-boiler, a full fledged novel suddenly seemed like a possibility. He could be the writer he was meant to be. As he wrote, he got engrossed in his own story and his hand reached out to the glass filled with vodka. This is the last one, he fooled himself.

***

Paws did not return. Anuj had gone around the block to look for her first thing that morning. Any flicker of hope had died out. He hadn't encountered either Randy or his neighbour either, which was a good thing as he wasn't sure how he would have reacted if he did. In his concern for Paws, he even forgot to check on the story he had written. But now, on his way home, he was eager to see if the plan had worked. The newspaper lay waiting in anticipation at the doorstep as he turned the keys. Anuj rifled through the pages, walking towards his room. Disappointment gnawed at him, the pages may well have been blank, nothing caught his eye.

He flung himself on the bed and curled his fingers over the phone, it was ringing with determination. Anuj ignored it, certain that it was Jay, curious to know if the plan had worked. He thought he would call him back after checking the laptop but the phone kept ringing till it hit voicemail. Anuj's heart froze as he heard the Inspector leave a message asking him to drop by at the police station for urgent questioning. It was his name, loud and clear, there was no mistake.

With dread, he read the carefully laid out story that he and Jay had plotted, the one he had typed with great conviction the previous night. And not a single word matched what he had written.

"The police got an anonymous call from a man tipping them off on the murderer. The man gave multiple clues to his identity. The key information was that he wrote the daily column at a popular newspaper. Thereon it was child's play for the police. They got the name and phone number from the office. The description of Anuj K Das matched the profile of the man as described by witnesses. The police called him up for questioning the very next morning."

Anuj called Jay in panic but it was switched off. He felt helpless and lost. Running from room to room he looked out the windows, and listened through the door. Not quite sure what he was expecting to see or hear, he acted in a senseless manner, driven by terror.

He knew he couldn't go to the police, he had no excuse or alibi. Anuj had interacted with the girl that day and it would be on the supermarket cameras. And it made no sense to even mention the drunken writing, it would only create more trouble. Despite wanting to desperately connect with Jay, he switched off his phone. He couldn't afford to get any more calls from the police or anyone else for that matter.

Anuj took a deep breath and tried to calm his nerves and clear his head. He had to save himself somehow. He decided to not write at all today, then there would be no further story. It was his damned writing that had started it all in the first place. As he paced around the house, he felt certain about his decision to not write. Up until he passed by the window by the tree.

She lay nestled among the twisted bare branches. He would have taken her for being fast asleep if not for the thick blood clot around her neck. The fact that the tree's branches only spread across his window and the neighbour's did not escape his attention. Before he could even open his window to reach out to his dear Paws, an eagle swooped in and carried her away.

All hell broke loose in Anuj's mind. Paws, Randy, the new neighbour, the pretty girl, all formed a pile of puzzle pieces that refused to fall into place. But he was beyond the desire to understand what was happening. The pain of the last few days was slowly turning into rage. The helplessness was giving way to an unknown strength born out of pain. The clutter gave way to clarity. All he knew was that Paws was dead. The police were after him. And somehow his writing was the culprit in all of this.

He realised that not writing further was not an option. Things had already been set into motion. He was already a suspect in the eyes of the police. The important thing right now was to get them off his back. The real killer was too close for comfort and had to somehow be exposed and captured before any more harm was done. And only he could do something about it.

After considerable deliberation, Anuj devised yet another plan. But this time he had a good feeling about it. He felt it would work, he felt it in his gut. The strategy was to write the story in an email to himself and then copy-paste it from there in one shot so that he had control over what he had written. It wouldn't even take long, so there would be no scope for modification. And he decided that he would certainly not get drunk. Just one drink to get him started. Then he would save the document and shut down the laptop. Remove the wire, having drained the battery earlier on. He would do everything he could to ensure that the writing did not get altered.

With uncanny confidence, he sat and wrote the email. All bases were covered. He mentioned that the killer was overcome by guilt and grief. He went to the police to confess his crime and gave details of how he had committed the murder, the time and place. How he had known the girl and why he had killed her. And then at the end, Anuj wrote the most important part, that the police jailed the true culprit for the murder.

After double checking, Anuj sent the mail to himself. As he waited for the battery to drain, he emptied all the liquor bottles that were hidden away in the house. The many rainy day options that he always ensured he had. Only two pegs were kept ready at the table in two shot glasses.

He paced the house, did odd jobs while waiting it out. Cleaned out long pending closets, put his clothes for a wash, and cleared out cobwebs that had started forming the day he had moved in. Finally, as the laptop reached minimum charge, he sat at the table. The two shotglasses beckoned him, he grabbed one, and quickly downed it. Shaking his head as the liquor burnt his throat, Anuj opened his mailbox and the word document. After clearing all that was on it from before, he copied the lines from the e-mail and pasted them into the document.

He did not feel drunk. There was no feeling of satisfaction either. He felt like he hadn't cleared his name yet and decided to add just another couple of lines, just to make it watertight.

"The police found no evidence against Anuj K Das. Clearing his name completely, they let him go scot-free."

Pleased with this final touch, he raised his second drink as toast and gulped it down. His nerves started to calm down and he waited for the laptop to shut down as the battery died, staring at the dark screen. To make things certain, he took out the wire, cut it into pieces, and threw them out of the window. Shutting the window tight, he hopped into bed. A crushing wave of exhaustion fell upon him and he drowned in deep sleep.

***

Anuj's eyes opened as day broke and sunlight barged in from the window. He had forgotten to pull the curtains. He sat up in bed feeling surprisingly fresh that morning and realised that he remembered everything from last night. Cautious confidence lit up inside him. It had worked, at last!

He switched his phone on and checked for calls and messages. There was nothing, from the police, from Jay, or anyone at all. Anuj walked around his apartment in a trance, every nook and corner. The streets lay empty. Randy's car sat silently by the curb. He stepped out his front door to check on the neighbour. The dark brown door stared back at him wordlessly. In a rush to read the newspaper, he grabbed it clumsily and it slipped to the floor. All the pages fell out and got mixed up. He bunched them up and took them to the sofa to sort them out.

Taking a deep breath, he allowed himself a smile. He felt proud and ridiculous at the same time, unable to believe he had gotten out of this mess and more so the incredulity of the mess. As he got the pages all in order, he finally flipped to the front page and read the headline. The whole front page was full of news on the deals the Prime Minister had struck on his recent foreign tours.

No police. No killer. No confession.

Anuj felt relaxed enough to get back to his routine morning cup of coffee. Things seemed to be going back to normal, the new normal. He opened the windows, flinching for a moment at the memory of a lifeless Paws seared into his mind. But he pushed the pain away, he had to look ahead. Things were falling into place. In the right direction. Sinking back into the sofa, he cupped his hands around the hot coffee mug, and closed his eyes. Only to open them wide instantly.

His eyes strayed back to the work table in his room, visible through the half ajar door. The laptop lay open on it. The screen was on and flickered inconsistently. The coffee spilled all over the floor as Anuj dropped his mug while reaching for the papers again. With trembling hands he kept going back and forth, unable to focus.

Finally, he stopped. There it was, his picture on the fourth page, where his column would normally be. He read the words written below.

"Killer strikes again. Anuj K Das, twenty eight years of age, a professional column writer with this very newspaper, was found dead in his apartment. His throat had been slit mercilessly, blood was all over the floor.....!"

Anuj threw the paper to the floor. He couldn't read any further. That was when he spotted the date on the newspaper and his feet turned to jelly. It was for the next day. A look of defeat on his face, he stared silently at the laptop on the table. As his heartbeat grew louder and faster the doorbell rang. And a deep voice called out menacingly. "Open the door Anuj!"

∿

LIFE

I sprouted a few branches or was it a pair of legs
I could travel the land now
Yet I wanted to fly!

I sprouted some more, or arms they might be
I could touch everything now
Yet I wanted to grab and hold!

The wind, rain, and sun touched me
I continued to grow and bloom
Yet I wanted to reach for the stars!

The world felt like it belonged to me
And I felt like I belonged in return
Yet I wanted to be free!

In the end I stayed where I was

I did not fly, I grabbed no one

The stars weren't mine, nor was freedom

I thought I was a human

Yet I lived like a tree!

Acknowledgements

I am grateful to everyone.

A special thanks to Rohit for the cover design!

www.ingramcontent.com/pod-product-compliance
Lightning Source LLC
Chambersburg PA
CBHW051235130726
47988CB00001B/360